Tijara's Heart

Book Four

F.T. Barbini

First Edition
First Printing, 2015
ISBN-10: 1940992141
ISBN-13: 978-1-940992-14-3

Koru Books is an imprint of Oloris Publishing.

Contact Oloris Publishing at info@olorispublishing.com. For more information please see: www.olorispublishing.com.

Acknowledgments

To Robert S. Malan, my calm within the storm.

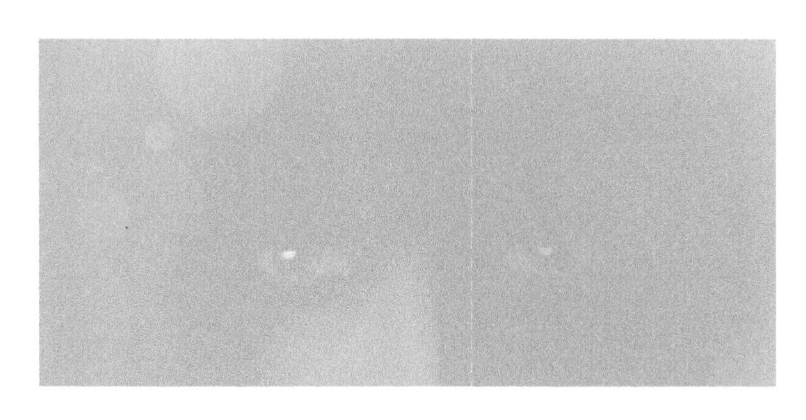

Contents

To Clara and Leonardo at Lido Garda,
where Big decisions are made.
And to Simon Radcliffe and Colin Orr,
heroes of the Public Libraries
and amazing supporters of my dreams.

PROLOGUE

Carlos Freja ended the vidcall with a pained expression on his face. He had been dialling his sister Clelia's number every day for the past five months, and watched the vidmessage on her answer-phone, fully aware that she wouldn't be picking up. Her house had been empty ever since the 19th of March 2858: the day humanity had completely disappeared from Earth. Calling her was neither logical nor rational, but seeing her warm smile had kept him going during that long summer, as he set about organising the largest rescue mission Zed had ever planned. Freja needed his own hope to remain strong; the hope that he would be able to find three billion people still alive and bring them home safely. His students would be counting on him, as too would Clelia. If only he knew where to start looking.

He stood up and strolled over to the only window in his office. He could see Tijara's entrance from there, with its luscious ferns crawling over the walls, and the gurgling blue waters of the surrounding moat. A group of 2 Mizki Juniors were waiting on the Intra-Rail platform, probably heading to Satras. Normally they would have been in class at this hour, but the start of term had been rescheduled to allow for all the preparations. He was going to miss this place, he thought.

A beep made Freja turn. 'Come in.'

The office door slid quietly open and Master Cress entered and bowed to the Tijaran Grand Master.

Freja bowed back and invited him to sit on one of the grey leather sofas. 'Coffee, Nathan?'

'Industrial strength, please.'

Freja poured two cups from the freshly filled pot and handed one to Cress, as the intoxicating aroma spread through the room. 'Let's hear it,' he said, sitting down.

'Some good news at last. List says we'll be ready for departure by the end of September, now that we know how to use those Arneshian portals. It wasn't easy to hack into their operational systems, but we've managed it. It means that when we find our people we can teleport them back here.'

Freja nodded, satisfied. He still couldn't believe that teleportation was actually possible, but it also didn't surprise him in the least that the Arneshians had discovered it; after all, they had been born with advanced technological skills. 'What else?'

'We've managed to replicate the static field they used against our fleet, back in March. It still needs to be properly studied, but we know it can stop anything in its tracks. Plus, we can create a protective cloak with it.'

'Excellent,' said Freja. 'We can activate it around Earth and use it to reinforce our own shield, here on Zed. We don't know how long we'll be gone for and I don't want to find any surprises when we get back.'

'On that note, List has requested to stay behind. He says someone has to work the main portal at this end.'

'Agreed. Tell him to assemble his team and pass on any other requests. I also want someone to check that our animals on Kapaldi 22 don't go killing each other off while we're away — at least not any more than nature intended.'

'How long do you think we'll be away for?'

'It's five months from here to Arnesh, at warp speed. Then we need to find our people, and who knows where we'll be by then. And let's not forget our *other mission*.'

Cress looked suddenly tense. 'Do you still intend to rebuild Tijara's Heart?'

'I do.' Freja's mood darkened a little. 'We don't have any time left. Salgoria will overwhelm us if we don't act now.'

'The Curia has agreed then?'

'Yes: on the condition that I build the crystal too, which was also my requirement.'

'The crystal ... how do we know it'll work this time? McCoy could–'

'It *will work,*' Freja cut in. 'We have no choice. We waited three years ... and for what? Our people have gone and it's our duty to find them; at all costs.' He stood up and walked back to the window. The warmth of the artificial sun soothed his skin and restored some sense of calm in him. 'These students are the best humanity has to offer, Nathan, and McCoy is the brightest star of them all. We *have to take the risk. If he can't do it, no one can.*'

'Does he need to know?' asked Cress, standing.

'Not until the time comes. Everything will be ready by then.'

'Very well,' said Cress.

As he left Freja's office, Cress felt the pressure of what was to come settling heavily on his heart. Still, he knew he would cope with it, as he had always done. But this time was different, because his anxiety came from the knowledge that Julius McCoy had just been chosen as Tijara's next sacrifice.

CHAPTER 1

MOONRISING

The crate sailed smoothly through the air, taking a sharp right turn at the centre of Tijara's hangar and headed straight for the west side, where dozens of similar containers were already neatly stacked against the wall. As it reached the top layer of them, it hovered there for a few seconds, then floated slightly to the left.

Julius McCoy was adjusting the crate's angle with his mind — an operation that he had performed at least four dozen times that morning — his right hand stretched out toward it, holding it suspended in midair. Once he was satisfied with its positioning, he gently lowered it into place and let out a sigh of relief.

'Excellent, mate,' said Faith, hovering over to him with the aid of his metal skirt. 'That was the last one.'

'For now,' said Julius, rubbing his temples. Using mind-skills for long periods of time always gave him a slight headache, even after three years of training.

'Then let's go grab some lunch. Me stomach is a-rumbling.'

Julius plucked his jumper up from the floor and dusted it off, paying particular attention to the new label on the left sleeve, which had "Julius McCoy – 4MA – Tijara" emblazoned on it in silver letters.

When the two boys arrived in the mess hall, they saw various small groups of students having their lunches and talking quietly among themselves. It was in stark contrast to the excited mealtime chatter of previous years. Julius had grown used to the dampened atmosphere of that summer and found it quite understandable considering the circumstances: loved ones, family members, friends — every last one of them had suffered during their latest encounter with the Arneshians, whisked away in the blink of an eye, victims of their enemy's technological superiority. Still, Julius was sure each of his fellow students hung from his same thread of hope: that somehow they would see them all again.

The Nuarns — later generations of Arneshians who had been raised on Earth — had been taken too, including Julius' own brother, Michael. What made it worse for Julius was that Michael, unlike his parents, had decided to leave Earth of his own free will, long before the Arneshians' final move; like 50 million other Nuarns, he thought that he was going *home*, to live with his own kind. If only they had listened to Zed's warnings about accepting the Arneshians' invitation, everything would have been different. But the Academy's words had fallen on deaf ears, and by the time the truth had been uncovered for all to see, it had been too late: earthlings and Nuarns alike had realised their mistake from the inside of an enemy ship.

Julius hated it when his thoughts took a trip of their own, revisiting the unpleasant events of the 19th of March, the day he had been unable to stop Ambassador T'Rogon from carrying out his plan, and when he had fought K'Ssander, the Arneshian boy, almost to the end. If Captain Kelly hadn't arrived when he had, Julius could have killed K'Ssander. 'Would have,' he thought to himself. 'He had Skye in a headlock and wasn't going to let him go. I gave him plenty of chances. What did he think, that I would let my friend get hurt without a figh–'

'Julius!' called Morgana, from a nearby table. 'Over here.'

He snapped back to the present and turned around. Faith had already been served and was sitting by Morgana's side, eating, while Julius was still standing, daydreaming at the counter, with an empty tray in his hands. He grabbed a plate of boiled carrot sticks and went to join them.

'Did you fall asleep or something?' asked Faith, amused.

'Just tired, that's all,' he answered.

Morgana looked at him, a concerned expression on her face. 'Still not sleeping?'

'On and off.' He nibbled half-heartedly on a carrot. 'It's all so different this year. No Summer Camp, no new timetables, no 1MJs to fill up the -6 dorm.'

'Aye, that's the creepiest thing,' said Morgana. 'All three schools are short of 30 students each — it's hard to believe there's no kids left.'

'I never thought I would say this,' added Faith, 'but I miss me classes. Especially Professor De Boer's. The only thing they've done so far is to insert those shield-chip implants into our feet, back in June. And they still hurt!'

'I wish they'd tell us something,' said Julius, feeling peeved. 'All we do is pack, move cargo and prep the fleet, but what's the plan?'

'I hear you,' said Faith. 'Personally I could do with a date.'

'And it would be about time too!' said Skye, arriving as if on cue and dumping himself on the bench next to Faith.

'Mr Miller,' said Faith, shifting to try make some space for himself. 'What an honour to see you.'

'I know, right,' he replied, stealing one of Julius' carrots. 'I'm telling you, I feel like I'm getting to know the Curia more intimately than I ever would have thought possible.'

'What?' said Julius. 'Is that your roundabout way of saying you've scored with Roversi's daughter already?'

'Nah. I've decided that going after the Curio Maximus' most prized possession could be a career breaker.'

'Or maker,' added Morgana. 'You could marry her, you know?'

Skye shivered. 'Don't even go there. Anyway, Faith, what's with the date request, then?'

'It's not *that* kind of date,' said Julius. 'We just want to know when the action is going to start.'

'And I have an answer for you,' replied Skye, winking.

'For real?' asked Julius, suddenly fully awake.

'Yep. But you guys can't tell anyone, ok? It'll be on the news later, anyway.'

'When?' urged Faith and Morgana in unison.

'28th of September.'

'In two days?' cried Julius.

'Shhh!' said Skye, hushing him and looking around nervously. 'I don't want to lose my future job!'

'This is awesome,' said Julius, lowering his voice. 'So what are they saying at the Curia?'

'I don't know where we're going — or how — but apparently they've found a lead as to where some of our people may be.'

'How did they do it?' asked Morgana, her food forgotten.

'Not sure, but it's what has kept us back this whole time. At least Gabriel List and his men have been able to work that teleportation thingy.'

'Wow,' said Faith. 'That technology is really something else. Sorry Skye, but when it must be said, it must.'

They all knew how Skye's hatred for everything Arneshian made him pretty touchy about anything resembling a compliment to them, so they simply avoided discussing how good their enemy's scientific knowledge was.

'It's fine,' he said. 'This is way too big to ignore. Did you know that List is staying behind, to activate the Zed portal?

'No way,' said Julius. 'I didn't think Freja would leave anyone behind.'

'Someone has to, though,' said Morgana, assertively, 'for when our people return.'

'Who else is staying, Skye?' asked Faith.

'Part of the Curia, a few medics, Gassendi's crew and most of Satras.'

'And what about us? What will they want us to do?'

'Not sure yet, but all the schools are going. Believe me, we won't be idle. The whole fleet is coming with.'

'I'm glad my sister Kaori is still in school,' said Morgana. 'All her older friends have already been given active duties.'

'That's right,' said Skye. 'Maya, from last year's Zed Toon, graduated in May and she's been assigned to one of the Herons.'

'She'll be fine, I'm sure,' added Morgana, noticing how his brow creased.

'Sure. I bet you're glad that your Maks is still in school. You guys going out, or what?'

She nodded enthusiastically, half blushing.

Julius coughed and almost choked on one of his carrots.

'*I knew it*,' continued Skye, cheekily. 'I saw you the other night in Satras, by the lake.'

'Really?' she said, fully blushing this time. 'Where were you?'

'Just passing by. I would have stopped to say hi too, if it wasn't for the fact that I couldn't actually see his hands?'

'Get out of here,' she said, giggling.

Even Faith began to laugh, as Morgana turned ever redder.

Julius, on the other hand, was only pretending — badly — to enjoy the banter. Inside his head, he was watching an image of himself wrecking the mess hall, dragging Maks Suraev by the hair, to behind the food counter, opening the oven door and throwing him inside, before shutting the door and raising the temperature to the max. Over the last couple of months he had managed to push his half-feelings for Morgana — with no small amount of effort — to the very back of his mind. Still, he really didn't need all this talk of "*your* Maks" and "disappearing hands" in the same sentence as "Morgana".

'Look at her, Jules,' said Skye. 'Isn't it funny how red she gets?'

'Hilarious,' he mumbled, renewing his attack on the carrot sticks.

'Speaking of ... this stuff,' said Faith, looking serious, 'and I may be totally off base here, but I think that ... maybe ... perhaps Siena likes me ... a little?'

The other three stared at him in perfect silence for a few seconds, and then started to laugh.

'What?' asked Faith, blushing every bit as red as Morgana had.

'I never thought I would see the day,' cried Skye, slapping his thigh.

'Bah ... you're probably right, I am mad,' he added sheepishly. 'I mean, I can't even walk.'

'No, no, no!' said Morgana, putting one hand on his arm. 'Quite the contrary. We're laughing because she's fancied you for ages, hovering skirt and all!'

'Does she?' he asked, eyes growing wide.

It took the best part of lunch to convince Faith that they weren't kidding, but when they returned to work that afternoon, he was sporting the most delighted smile they had seen in a long time.

By that evening, rumours of the impending departure had been officially confirmed, lifting the mood right across Zed. All the Mizkis received a message to gather in the assembly hall by 10:00 hours of the following morning, for a short briefing. So it was that, after a late breakfast, Julius arrived at the hall with his classmates, and waited eagerly for the Grand Master's appearance.

The empty rows at the back were a painful reminder of the absence of the 1MJs and sure enough, when Freja entered, Julius noticed him glancing sadly at those very seats. The Mizkis stood up as Freja climbed the four steps to the podium. As he bowed in acknowledgement to them, they bowed back.

'Be seated,' he said.

It occurred to Julius that Freja looked in much higher spirits today than he had over the course of the summer. The Tijaran Grand Master, who had been busy with preparations, had occasionally appeared on the Space Channel, always looking tired and strained. But not today, thought Julius. Today, he looked as strong as the first time he had seen him, right there in that same hall.

'Mizkis,' Freja began, 'for the past three years, the Lunar Perimeter has been at the centre of events that will live forever in history. After decades of seemingly peaceful existence, Queen Salgoria and her people twice tried, and failed, to shake our world, but succeeded in the end.' Freja let his words echo in the stillness of the hall. 'We have all suffered much these last few months, dealing with the loss of our families and friends, afraid that we would never know what became of them. When I think that I at least know where one of my family, my own son, is, I cannot help but feel a little guilty, knowing that most of you sitting here before me have no such luck.'

'He has a son?' whispered Julius into Skye's ear, but his friend looked just as surprised.

'You have all worked hard this summer, helping Zed prepare for its biggest ever mission, and for that I thank you. Mizkis, you have made us proud.'

Murmurs of assent broke the silence and Julius could have sworn he heard a few sniffles from the back.

'Tomorrow at noon,' continued Freja, 'we will leave the Moon and our own solar system. I cannot tell you when we will return, nor if all of us ever will but, wherever we go, we shall carry the legacy of Marcus Tijara with us.'

'On your feet, Mizkis!' cried Master Cress, who was standing a little behind, and to the right of Freja.

Julius was startled, as he hadn't noticed him entering the room. The ceiling began to retract and the lights dimmed. He looked up, as the vastness of space filled his view, separated only by the Zed shield. Then he saw a vast shadow, slowly obscuring the starlight.

'Behold the might of Moonrising!' declared Freja.

Julius' mouth formed an O, as a sense of awe fell over him.

'It's a battlestar ...' uttered Faith, mesmerised by the sight of it.

Towering over their heads was the most majestic spaceship that Julius had ever seen. Dark as the night, it reminded him of a shark, as viewed from below. It was exceptionally tall — *thick*, was the word that came to mind — and he was able to make out five distinct layers, which appeared as if they had been designed to fit snugly together, as they were now, but still able to separate when needed.

'Mizkis,' said Cress, 'let's hear it for our new home.'

Julius prepared for the school salute, pressing his right arm against his body, with his left hand resting on Skye's right shoulder.

Cress shouted, 'In your heart!'

Julius cried back, 'TI-JA-RA!' as he slammed his right fist against his chest and stomped his right foot on the ground, at the same time. Just like the first day he had done the salute, he felt a rush of energy fire through him.

Freja looked at the students. 'A new chapter of history lies before us. May we return home, victorious!'

'So let it be,' answered the assembly.

The Grand Master bowed and left the hall, while Master Cress took his place on the podium. The excitement was tangible, and it was a few minutes before silence could be restored.

'You will receive the blueprints for Battlestar Moonrising later today. Pack your belongings and say your goodbyes. Boarding procedures will commence tomorrow morning at 08:00 hours from the school's hangar. Dismissed!'

That afternoon Julius thought it only appropriate that the Skirts have one last game in the Hologram Palace before leaving. Unfortunately, it seemed every other student on Zed had the same idea, so they ended up having an ice-cream at Mario's Ice-land instead, before returning to the school to lounge in the garden, under their favourite oak tree.

'It says here that it can carry 5,000 people,' marvelled Faith, reading from the holoscreen floating over the palm of his hand.

'What's in each of its layers?' asked Julius, pulling himself closer to Faith.

'Tijara, Tuala and Sield schools are in the top three. Then one is shared by the Curia and the Hospital, and the last one is occupied by New Satras; says here it can carry 3,000 peeps by itself!'

'Not bad,' said Julius. 'That's why it looks massive.'

'When all the ships are together,' read Morgana from her own screen, 'they call it the Citadel, and hyperjump is offline.'

'Not warp, I hope,' remarked Faith.

'That one's fine. But all units must split before a skip.'

'And what about our fleet?' asked Skye, lying on the grass, staring up at the oak's long and luscious branches.

'There will be Cougars onboard each hangar,' answered Morgana, quickly retrieving the information. 'Plus a fleet of Herons, 10,000 strong.'

'Talk about the solitude of space,' said Julius, impressed by the numbers.

'Hey guys,' said Skye, 'I picked up something for us to mark the occasion.'

'Is it legal?' asked Faith.

'Come closer,' he said, and knelt next to the oak's trunk.

Julius watched as Skye pulled a small metal plaque from his pocket, together with his trusty Omni-gizmo which was currently on its screwdriver setting. He held the plaque against the tree and fixed it to the wood. Selecting the laser setting next, he proceeded to write, "The Skirts were here" on it, followed by his own name.

'I didn't think you were the sentimental type,' said Faith, taking the gizmo from Skye's hand and etching his name below his.

Julius and Morgana followed suit, adding their names as best they could.

'That was a lovely idea, Skye,' said Morgana.

Julius thought so too. At least there was some mark of them having been there, left behind. After all, no matter how mighty Moonrising had looked to him, there was no guarantee they would return victorious, as Freja had wished. Even with all the optimism in the universe, there was still a chance they may not return at all.

CHAPTER 2

THE NEW SOLO CHAMPION

Leaving Tijara had not been easy for Julius, who had been surprised by the sense of loss he had felt that morning. For months he had been waiting for the rescue mission to begin, without sparing much thought to what he would be giving up by leaving. He stared at his school through the Stork's small porthole window, as it disappeared slowly from view below him, lost in the shimmering waves of Zed's shield. 'I wonder if we'll make it back for graduation,' he said, quietly.'

Faith followed his gaze out to the Moon. 'You think it'll take us that long?'

'Who knows,' he answered. 'But if it does ... then today was the last time we'll ever get to wake up in Tijara. We can't go back once we're officers.'

'I hadn't thought about it,' said Faith. 'You're making me sad, McCoy. And I don't want to be sad on me birthday week. Already I feel like there's not a lot to celebrate.'

'Sixteen is a good one, Faith,' said Julius. 'At the very least let us take you to New Satras for some food.'

'All right, but no Supernova, please,' he added quickly, remembering the stomach-bursting cake they had got for him on his previous birthday. 'I think me guts are still suffering last year's side effects.'

'Yeah,' grinned Julius, 'Nurse Primula mentioned your *indisposition*.'

'I never wished so badly to be a cow, like I did that night, McCoy. I tell you, I could have really done with an extra stomach.'

Julius laughed. 'Did you wish to be a cow on more than one occasion? Don't worry mate, no cake for you this year.' With his mood uplifted, Julius readied himself for boarding Moonrising.

The anticipation of the impending mission had spread throughout the Mizkis, renewing their hope and strengthening their hearts. Julius could see thick wisps of green and grey floating below the ceiling, a sign of their excitement, mixed in with a twinge of anxiety. By the time the Stork docked inside the battlestar, the wisps were filling the entire shuttle.

'This place is bigger than Pete's'!' cried Faith, hovering into the hangar without even bothering to pick his bag up.

When she heard that, Morgana rushed outside, leaving Julius and Skye to carry all of their stuff.

'Here we go again,' said Julius, shrugging and shouldering her rucksack.

Skye shook his head and picked up Faith's. 'Some things never change.'

As it was, the hangar was much larger than Julius had imagined, with high ceilings, mezzanines, gangways and plenty of wide, open spaces. As he walked towards the exit, he passed row upon row of black Cougars, silently waiting, like animals ready to pounce; he knew there were even more of them in the levels above and below him, without counting those carried by the other two schools. Including the thousands of Herons following them, Zed was really travelling with a mighty fleet this time. And that, Julius kept thinking, was bound to help. On leaving the hangar, he saw a large screen on the wall, with the full layout of Tijara. He quickly noticed familiar flashing red dots set into the walls, and figured that they were there to direct them to the central section of the ship where, no doubt, the dorms, galley, mess hall and engine room were located. To the left of this were the bridge and the War-deck, plus the staff and officers' quarters; to the right were the training areas for the White and Grey Arts classes.

'How do we get to New Satras?' called out Lopaka, a question which was promptly echoed by most of his classmates.

'Wouldn't you like to know, Mr Liway,' Hamza Patel answered cheerily. The guidance teacher of the Mizki Apprentices had just joined them and was now motioning for them to follow him.

As they trooped after Patel, Julius tried to keep track of their route, but each new corridor looked the same as the previous one, with dull, grey metal features everywhere. The whole vessel felt weird: it lacked the cosiness of the Ahura Mazda and the comforts of Gea One. Maybe it was just the sheer size of it, or perhaps it was just its nature — after all, Moonrising *was* a battleship. In one word, Julius would have described it as *gritty*.

Eventually, after numerous turns and sets of stairs, they arrived at their dorms.

'3MAs,' called Patel, 'left corridor. 4MAs, to the right. Girls' rooms first, then boys, same pairs as always. Drop your belongings and meet me back here in five minutes. Go!'

The Mizkis shuffled along, filing into their respective corridors. Julius and Skye headed to their room, which, like on Zed, was the third one on the right.

Skye looked into the retina sensor and the door slid open silently. 'This is shabby as anything,' he said, trudging over to the further of the two beds in the room.

Julius dropped his bag on the floor and looked around. There were no windows, but the wall had one large scenery screen, which also acted as a display. The room was certainly smaller than what they usually had, but he didn't figure he would be spending much time there anyway.

'The bathroom is tiny,' said Skye, peering into a back room. 'I hope Faith can fit in his one, with his skirt.'

'Surely they've thought of that,' said Julius, heading for the door. 'Come on. Let's get going.'

As it turned out, Faith was more than satisfied with his extra-large facilities, an unexpected benefit which made his roommate Barth a very happy Mizki indeed.

Once all the Apprentices were back, Patel led them up the stairs, into the mess hall.

'This is a bit ... dismal,' groaned Morgana, miserably observing the shabby grey decor all around.

Julius was sure he was going to have to change his one word description of Moonrising from *gritty* to *depressing*. 'Did they run out of money or something?'

'Please, let the food be all right,' added Skye, sounding concerned.

Julius, who was now feeling particularly grumpy, took a seat on one of the hard, iron benches. 'If this is it, I'm not looking forward to seeing New Satras at all,' he muttered.

Patel was waiting for the students to sit, all the time observing them with an amused little smile. 'Welcome to BM Tijara, Mizkis,' he began. 'I trust you found your dorms welcoming and cheerful.'

'Has he *seen* the dorms?' whispered Morgana.

'The stylish interior design,' continued Patel, 'is especially visible in common areas, such as this mess hall. The vibrancy of the colours simply jumps out at you, doesn't it?'

'Is he even on the same ship as us?' said Leanne Nord, not quietly enough.

Patel seemed to be greatly enjoying their puzzlement, until he could no longer disguise it and began to laugh.

'That's it,' said Faith, 'he's banged his head somewhere. Julius, get Nurse Primula.'

'I'm sorry, Mizkis,' said Patel, regaining some composure. 'What you see is a battlestar in safe mode, where all power is converged in its core. This can happen during hyperjump or in combat. Normally though, part of the power is re-routed to the holonet, which makes this place feel a little more homely.'

Julius was still unsure about how that would actually work, but three years on Zed had, if nothing else, taught him to expect the improbable.

'MAs,' said Patel. 'I give you the *real* Moonrising.'

At those words a wave of crackling static shot through the room, striking across every single surface in the mess hall. As it passed over, it laid a kaleidoscope of colours across the furniture, floor, ceiling and walls, transforming the dreary hall into a first class lounge area.

'Plug me in and call me a floor lamp,' said Faith, hovering upwards and twirling on the spot in delight as he admired the changes.

Julius was every bit as astonished as everyone else at what he saw. Thanks to the soft wall lights, the atmosphere had been transformed into something far more relaxed: pastel tones of blue and green helped with the new uplifting ambience of the place, while leafy virtual plants lent the sitting areas an air of privacy and comfort.

Patel enjoyed the Mizkis' reaction a little longer, before regaining their attention. 'Given the circumstances we find ourselves in, the school year will revolve around the rescue mission. Your timetables will be reduced to only the essentials and, most importantly, it will be flexible. Some of your teachers are on active duties, like Professor Farshid, so, when they're needed, your classes will be cancelled at a moment's notice. That said, there is a weekly programme of studies for all of you, which will be sent to your PIPs.'

'We'd completely understand if you happened to forget to do that,' added Faith, innocently.

'Thank you, Mr Shanigan. I'll make sure I *don't* forget,' replied Patel, drawing a few laughs from the students. 'Teachers or not, you still need to complete your training.'

'Good try, Faith,' said Julius, patting him on the shoulder.

'And now, for your timetables.' Patel activated his PIP and dabbed the screen a few times. 'Open your mail, please.'

A moment later Julius received Patel's message and opened it. He quickly saw that his chosen subjects – Spaceship Management and Catalyst training – were on Monday and Wednesday mornings.

'Here's the new subject,' cried Skye excitedly. 'It's called Twist.'

'Wait,' said Julius. 'Isn't that like, an old dance?'

'I doubt it's the same thing,' said Morgana. 'It's says here that Professor Morales will be taking it.'

'Followed by an hour of Gene Therapy for yours truly,' added Julius.

'They're still playing with your DNA, huh?' asked Faith, leaning in to examine his planner.

'Apparently so,' replied Julius, who wasn't too happy about it.

'Better you than me.'

'Cheers.'

'It looks like Fridays are free,' said Skye.

Julius checked and noticed the empty space. The weekly programme seemed greatly reduced compared to previous years — not that he minded that too much.

Patel allowed them a few minutes to examine the message, then spoke again. 'Until 17:00, Monday to Friday, you must remain within Tijara, as you could be assigned to internal active duties. Outside of these times, you are free to visit New Satras although, for this week, you must wait until Saturday morning. Curfew is at the usual 20:00, Sunday to Thursday, and 21:00 at weekends. As for today, you'll start your timetable at 14:00.'

'Do we still need to keep a log of each lesson?' asked Isolde, clearly hoping for a negative answer.

'You do, Miss Frey,' he said, shattering that little dream. 'And now you're free to go.'

With lunchtime approaching, Julius and the others decided to remain in the hall, and moved over to a group of sofas, where they were soon joined by Siena and Isolde.

At one point Morgana nudged Julius in the ribs, and pointed at Faith, a cheeky grin on her face. When Julius looked up he saw that Faith was peering at Siena through the transparent holoscreen on his hand, pretending to read something.

'*Caught you!*' said Julius, inside Faith's mind.

Faith jolted, and fumbled with his screen, clearly flustered.

Julius and Morgana tried to stifle a laugh as Faith attempted to reactivate his PIP as if nothing had happened, all the time throwing them daggers with his eyes.

Just as Julius was returning to examine his class schedule, Gustavo Perez's voice rang through the mess hall. 'Blimey, McCoy! Have you seen the Solo chart?'

The whole room went quiet and, judging by Gustavo's face, it was easy to tell that it wasn't good news.

Julius removed the timetable from the screen with a flick of his finger and selected the Game Charts app. Without realising it, he was now literally on the edge of his seat and his palms had grown sweaty. After almost two years as the reigning Solo champion of Zed, another Mizki had beaten Julius: appearing at rank 1 was the unknown F.H., from Sield School. He re-read the chart again, just to make sure he had it right, but no matter how many times he checked it, F.H. was still there, for a game played the evening before, during their last night on Zed. Julius was too stunned to say anything and largely ignored the sympathetic pats on the shoulder from his classmates.

By lunchtime, he was still staring blankly at the screen, so Morgana went to fill his tray for him, while Faith and Skye led him by his arms to the table. Julius was processing the news, while having his food, which quite clearly wasn't happening, as he demonstrated by trying to eat his soup with a fork.

'Are you all right?' asked Morgana tentatively.

'Here, mate,' said Skye, handing him a spoon. 'You'll never finish it at this rate.'

Julius stared blankly at the spoon, then at Skye, then stood and banged his fists on the table. 'How could I let that happen?' he cried in frustration. 'Aaargh!' And with that, he strode off in a huff, returned to the table to grab a pork rib before storming off again, leaving the Skirts in resigned perplexity.

'What just happened?' asked Professor Chan, passing by the table, carrying a tray.

'Someone beat him at Solo,' answered Skye. 'A certain F.H., from Sield.'

Chan laughed. 'Ah! Imagine his face when he finds out that he was beaten by a girl! No offence, Miss Ruthier.'

'None taken,' she replied.

As soon as Chan had gone, they looked at each other, mouths gaping.

'Morgana,' said Skye, 'ask Maks who she is. Come on!'

She quickly sent Maks a message, begging him for a reply as soon as possible.

During pilot training that afternoon, Julius went through the motions, unable to focus and not even realising that Moonrising had just broken orbit. Luckily Professor Clavel had asked them to do some revision on Cougar maintenance, which meant that he simply had to stare at the manual in order to appear busy.

The news that F.H. was a girl had spread through Tijara like wildfire and, by dinner time that evening, Maks had replied to Morgana, confirming that her name was Farrah Hendricks, a 4MA. More than that, he didn't know, as she had only joined Sield that year.

Just when Julius thought that it couldn't get any worse, his PIP beeped. The message was short and to the point: 'Meet me in New Satras, Rowan Square; Sat at noon. Bring the ring. Farrah XXX.'

Faith grabbed Julius' hand and turned it so he could read the message, then got the others at the table to lean and have a look. 'Oh no, not the *ring*,' he teased.

'Ouch!' said Skye. 'At least she signed off with three kisses.'

'Let me see that!' said Morgana, suddenly very curious. She grabbed his hand and pulled him halfway across the table.

'Steady there!' said Julius, trying to avoid her plate of mash. 'It's attached to me, remember.'

'You never know, McCoy,' said Skye, winking. 'Something good *can* come of this, you know.'

'Nonsense,' said Morgana, a little too loudly. Realising that they were all looking at her, she let go of Julius' hand. 'She's ... the enemy. Julius couldn't possibly fraternise with the enemy now, could he? It would look ... odd, so soon after he's lost.' Seeing as they were still staring at her, she stood up, flicked her black hair behind her shoulders and huffed, 'It's late. I'm going to bed.' And with that, she stormed off.

'I bet it's the hormones,' added Skye, as an afterthought. 'It'll pass.'

To Julius however, it felt more like a hint of jealousy which, in his mind, was the best news he had had all day.

On Tuesday morning, Julius arrived at breakfast sporting two big bags under his eyes, and carrying two mugs of black coffee.

'Rough night, huh?' asked Morgana, looking a lot more relaxed than the previous evening.

Julius nodded. 'And I deserve it too.'

'Why's that?' asked Faith, biting into his toast.

'Och, it's something Professor Gould told me last year in class,' explained Julius. 'He said that getting to the top isn't hard, but *staying* on top is. I've just proved his point.'

'Fair enough,' said Morgana. 'But you know, it's not like we've had a lot of time to play lately.'

'I know,' he said. 'It still sucks, though.'

'At least you can say you've been on that chart,' said Faith, brandishing the half eaten toast in his direction. 'Cheer up, mate.'

In the end, Julius had to let it go, or at least managed to push it to the back of his mind enough to face his first full day of lessons.

Returning to a routine felt oddly comforting to him. There was so much going on outside Moonrising — what with the mission, the concern over his family and friends and more potential attacks from the Arneshians — that the timetable gave him a sense of familiarity, of something that was safe.

Professor Lao-tzu invited the Mizkis to use his class on a Friday, to meditate, since with the pressure of possible combat situations, he wanted everyone to be as focused as they could. Morgana clapped cheerily at the news, meditation being one of her favourite pastimes.

'Guess where I'll *not* be on a Friday,' whispered Julius to Faith.

Unfortunately for Julius, however, there was no escaping the Tuesday morning hour in the infirmary, for his DNA augmentation, which he decided to pass with a cheeky snooze.

Professor Morales and Professor Chan helped the Mizkis learn how to use the latest shield implants. The students had found walking and fighting with two implants hard enough and it had taken them more than a year to master; now, they had to deal with four, two of which sprung out of their feet.

Morales showed them how these behaved differently from the chips in their arms: for one thing, they dissolved whenever they crossed one of their body parts or the upper shields — the sensors were programmed to recognise their owner's DNA — making their protection less reliable; on the other hand, they created a formidable barrier when the person was standing still, allowing them to protect an entire group efficiently.

Needless to say, Professor Chan planned their Martial Arts classes to include plenty of excruciating leg work. Even Faith wasn't exempt from this, as Chan taught him how to retract the bottom panels of his skirt, allowing him to use the shields in his feet as well.

As for Professor King, who was redder and jollier than ever, he had decided that, in celebration of them being on a battleship, they would hone their telekinetic skills by pushing Cougars along the runways.

'A *Cougar*?' cried Faith in astonishment. 'That spells hemorrhoids to me.'

Professor King found that remark hilarious and patted Faith on the shoulder hard enough to send him flying sideways, before demonstrating what to do on a nearby plane.

'I'll go retrieve Faith,' said Lopaka, quietly.

Julius nodded. 'Thanks mate.' He looked back at King, and shook his head. He had to admit, his teacher was as crazy as it got, but he was also very good. The Cougar began to roll along on its wheels slowly, but steadily, leaving a puzzled mechanic, who was lying flat on his back beneath the plane, holding his tools in midair, watching as the engine he was working on moved away from above his nose.

To complete what had proved to be a very full day, Professor Beloi — who had reached his forty-second birthday without uttering a single word — promised them stress, anxiety and more pressure for the rest of the year, as he discussed his plans for improving their telepathic skills.

All in all, it had been a busy day, thought Julius that night. But, as with every other 4MA, he was really looking forward to his first Twist lesson, and wondering what exactly he would be doing in it.

On Thursday morning, at 09:00, the Skirts, along with Siena, made their way to Morales' classroom. Mercifully, Skye had stopped wearing his awful aftershave, finally acknowledging that not only did it *not* attract Morales, but instead repelled every female in a 30 feet radius.

'Good morning, Mizkis,' greeted Morales, with a bow to the class. 'Sit, please.'

Julius sat down on the floor and watched as she casually retrieved three balls from the back of the room, using her mind-skills.

'From this year, we start training on the Sub-molecular Distortion Field — Twist, as we call it. So, how many of you have managed to unbind molecules before?'

Julius looked around him, and slowly raised his hand, hoping he wasn't the only one. To his surprise, George Lowet and Femi Mubarak also raised their hands.

'That's quite a number,' said Morales, sounding pleased. 'Normally, we have none. Can you tell us: what is the biggest object you have ever twisted, please?'

Femi answered, 'A plate, ma'am.'

'A pillow,' said George.

'Er ... a bathtub?' offered Julius, reddening slightly.

'Oh!' said Morales. 'Was anyone in it at the time?'

'Um ... yeah. My dad,' he admitted, shyly.

'I remember that!' said Morgana, laughing. 'That story went around the whole neighbourhood!'

'Very good, Mizkis,' continued Morales. 'Can you three come up here, please?'

Julius, Femi and George walked up to the centre of the room.

Morales bounced one of the balls a couple of times, then threw all of them up, froze them in midair with her mind, and said, 'Take one each and Twist it. On three.'

Julius stepped to the one closest to him and nodded at the other two, feeling a little nervous. The class had gone silent in anticipation, making him realise that some of them had never seen this skill in action before. He stretched his hand towards the ball and, on Morales' signal, he locked his mind on the ball and felt it ripping apart, as he envisioned the molecules being pulled in different directions.

The effect of the Twist made the class gasp. There were three soft thudding sounds, then the balls were reduced to thousands of tiny fragments, all suspended in front of the standing students.

'Where are the balls?' asked Barth, sounding suitably stupefied.

'Those *bits*, Mr Smit,' explained Morales, 'are the balls.' She turned to Julius. 'Can you re-bind them?'

'Sort of,' he answered, 'but not that well.'

Morales looked questioningly at Femi and George, who both shook their heads.

'Very well,' she said, stretching her hand towards the pieces; as they all watched in amazement, she bound them back together, into three solid balls once more. 'Thank you, Mizkis.'

There were a few cheers from their impressed classmates as they sat back down.

'There's a catch, however, with this particular mind-skill,' continued Morales. 'As you saw, your three colleagues can unbind molecules and keep them suspended, which means that, as well as practicing Twist, they will also focus on rebinding objects. In the meantime, though, I'll need to test everyone else and, if you don't have the Twist gene active in your DNA, I'm afraid you'll need to spend a few lessons with Doctor Walliser, who will unlock it for you.'

'Will we still be able to do it then?' asked Isolde, hopefully.

'Of course,' replied Morales. 'If you are here, then you are all carriers, Miss Frey. You may just need a little push in the right direction, is all. Besides, you wouldn't want to leave all the fun to these three, would you?'

Soon, Morales began testing the rest of the class. Julius, Femi and George stood to one side while she did this, watching as their classmates tried to unbind the ball, without a single one of them succeeding. By the end of the second hour, Morales had scheduled them all in for treatment with the doctor, starting from the following week.

'I knew they would find a way to send me to the infirmary again,' moaned Faith, as they left the room at the end of the class.

'At least you'll be done in a few weeks,' said Julius. 'I've got the *whole year* to spend in that place for my treatment. Speaking of, I'd better go. Catch you later.'

Saturday the 6th of October finally came around and, as Julius awoke that morning, he immediately remembered what lay ahead. Skye must have also remembered because, even before he was out of bed he said, 'Do you want us to come with you to meet Farrah?'

Julius thought about it for a moment. 'I'm fine, don't worry. I'll see you guys afterwards, for Faith's birthday lunch. What did we get him in the end?'

'The best present ever,' said Skye. 'A voucher for a session in the sim-dating programme.'

'No way!'

'It'll be awesome.'

'Just don't give it to him in front of Siena, please.'

'Good point. Let's make tracks, it's almost eleven o'clock and your date is in an hour.'

'It's *not* a date,' growled Julius, throwing his pillow at Skye, which hit him perfectly in the face.

'All right, I get it!' laughed Skye, hopping out of bed.

'You go first,' said Julius, pointing to the bathroom. As his friend went off to shower, he lay there, staring at the scenery screen, where an autumnal morning sun had replaced the starry darkness of space. The Solo ring on his finger felt cold to the touch; he was just about to pull it off, but hesitated. 'Just a little longer,' he said to himself.

At 11:30, Julius, Skye and Faith met Morgana and Siena at the rear exit of Tijara. There were three sets of lifts that linked each of the four layers of Moonrising: one at the front, one at the centre and one at the back, all of which were working at full capacity today. They managed to squeeze inside, despite having to fight for space with the other Mizkis, who were also anxious to see New Satras.

When the door opened, Julius was pushed out of the lift and against the side wall by a human wave. 'This reminds me of our first time in Satras,' he cried to Skye, who was stuck behind a boisterous group of Mizki Juniors.

Faith was happily hovering above the crowd, directing Morgana and Siena towards Julius.

'At least *he's* having fun,' said Skye, pointing at Faith, while trying to grab hold of Morgana's hand.

Julius couldn't go anywhere for the moment, so he flattened himself against a recess in the wall, using a nearby doorframe for shelter. As he did so, he heard a loud clicking noise and felt a strong sensation of heat against his neck. He jerked his head away and turned to face the door. Its surface was unremarkably flat, sporting only a single plaque in the centre of it which read, "TH – Off Limits" followed by a drawing of four stars — one at the top, two below it to either side, and one at the bottom — joined together by straight lines to form a diamond. Julius passed his fingers over the plaque, and was surprised to find that it was cold to the touch. 'Strange,' he thought.

'Over here, Julius!' called Faith.

'Coming,' he replied, leaving the door behind and joining his friends.

As they made it past the main entrance, they stopped in front of a large map of New Satras, which showed four floors of shops, bars and restaurants, with a holofloor that extended right down to level -5.

Julius checked the time and realised that he was going to be late. Quickly, he typed out "Rowan Square" on one of the information pads on the wall, and an area of level -3 lit up in green. 'I've got five minutes to get there, guys.'

'Want me to carry you?' volunteered Faith.

'That wouldn't do much for my dignity, but thanks.'

'Let's meet back here in one hour,' said Skye, pointing at a place on the map.

'*Eat Your Mama Blind*?' read Morgana. 'What kind of a place is that?'

'If they serve food,' said Skye, dragging her away, 'it's my kind of place, lady.'

'See you later, Julius,' she called, waving to him.

He waved back, then headed for the lower levels. He didn't have a lot of time to look around just then, but New Satras appeared to be a lot like a fancy shopping mall, very much like the ones they had back on Earth. It was certainly full of life and colour, but without the wide, open spaces of the real Satras.

When Julius arrived at level -3, he checked a nearby map and saw that Rowan Square was right at the centre of this floor. He hurried along the main path, and it suddenly dawned on him that he didn't even know what this girl looked like; secretly he hoped that he would miss her altogether, so he could keep the ring for a little longer: after all, Bernard Docherty had waited until the end of the year before he had passed it on to Julius.

As he reached Rowan Square, he quickly noted how it was the first green area he had seen so far in New Satras. The path opened up into a medium sized park, complete with wooden benches, grass and, unsurprisingly, numerous rowan trees. Julius wondered if they were real or just another trick of the simulator, but either way they looked good and made the place feel more alive. The scenery ceiling above the park showed a beautiful blue sky, further adding to the illusion of this being an outside area. Julius stepped onto the grass and strolled towards the big tree at the centre of the park, all the time playing nervously with the ring. He checked the time and saw that it was 12:05. There were a few Mizkis sitting on the benches, busily chatting or eating.

He expected that she would be alone or, at the very least, on the lookout for him too.

Just when he was about to give up and leave, he noticed a girl walking slowly across the grass, coming towards him. It is fair to say that, at that moment, Julius experienced a quite unexpected lowering of his jaw, which left him gawping for several seconds in a most unbecoming manner. Thankfully for him, she was still too far away to see this, giving him time to recompose himself, flatten his hair and straighten his clothes. He coughed, breathed in deeply, and leaned casually against the tree trunk. When she saw him, her lips formed the most beautiful smile and Julius almost slid off the trunk. With every step she took, her honey blonde hair danced around her shoulders, while her smooth skin seemed to reflect the light around her.

She stopped right in front of him and stretched out her hand. 'Farrah Hendricks.'

Julius simply stared back, wondering if he had ever seen eyes quite so blue before. He looked at her hand and, mustering all of his courage — more so, it seemed, than he had needed to face Red Cap — he grabbed hold of it with his own. 'Julius McCoy.'

She smiled and held his hand for a few moments, before letting go.

Julius decided that if he wanted to make it out of there without completely embarrassing himself, he would need to pull himself together double-quick. 'Coffee?' he asked her.

'Sure. There's a cart over there,' she pointed. 'Just black.'

Julius nodded and headed for the vendor, breathing deeply as he went. 'Don't screw this up, McCoy,' he said to himself.

When he returned, Farrah was sitting on the grass, her long legs gathered under her.

'Here you go,' he said, passing her the paper cup.

'Thanks.'

Getting the drinks had been a good idea, as Julius began to feel a bit more relaxed and in charge of his jaw. For some curious reason, he found himself wanting to make a good impression. He might have lost the Solo title, but he wasn't a *total* loss. 'I guess congrats are in order.'

She bowed her head, and smiled. 'I was really surprised when I saw the score, believe me.'

'How come your Solo video isn't out yet?'

'I don't know. Maybe a problem with the recordings?'

'Shame. I would have liked to see you in action.'

'Yours was pretty cool.'

'You mean you watched it?' said Julius, feeling a surge of pride at that.

'A lot,' she replied. 'You could say I've studied it thoroughly. I wanted to ask you so many things about it …'

'Why didn't you?' he said quickly, forgetting that they had only just met.

Farrah looked down and plucked delicately at a blade of grass. 'I wasn't well.'

'Oh,' he said. 'Is that why you weren't at school last year? I mean, my friend Maks told me you had just joined us.'

'That's right. I had to be in hospital for a while. My folks have a business on Satras so, when I wasn't ill, I stayed with them. Then, this summer, the doctors said I could try out for Sield and see if I managed to get in.'

'Well, you managed it all right,' said Julius. 'I mean, you come back to school and the first thing you do is steal the Solo title! I think I need to have a word with your doctor.'

'I'm so sorry,' she said, teasing him. As she laughed, she put her hand on Julius' arm, sending shivers all over his body.

'So, uh … were you, uh, *very* ill?' he stammered.

'I can't quite remember my time in hospital, to tell the truth. The doctor said it's a characteristic of my disorder.

I'm fine now though, but I still need to be checked every month or so.'

'You look … plenty healthy to me,' he added.

'Thank you. My mum would agree,' she said, cheerfully. 'She told me so just this morning.'

'Your parents are here, then?'

'Yes. One level above us,' she said, pointing up. 'Yours? Were they …?'

'Aye.'

'I'm sorry. How many of your family?'

'My folks, my granny, and my brother. He's a Nuarn actually, so he *chose* to go.' As those words left his lips, Julius realised just how easy it had been to tell her about Michael. He was rather surprised by that.

'Is that the Solo ring?' she said, tactfully changing topic.

'The very one,' answered Julius. He took it off, gave it a quick wipe with a corner of his t-shirt and held it up. 'I forgot the box.'

'It's OK. I'll wear it now, anyway,' she said holding her hand out to him.

Julius felt slightly awkward, but she was still smiling at him. So, for the second time that morning, he took her hand and put the ring on it.

The black band automatically adjusted to fit her finger. She held it to her heart, batted her eyelashes a few times, and sweetly sighed, 'Oh darling! But of course I accept!'

Julius panicked. 'What … No … I …'

'Got you!' she said, laughing. 'It'll take more than a ring to woo me. Hey, how about a picture to mark the occasion?'

He nodded, feeling slightly out of his depth and very much not in control of the situation once more. Farrah opened up her PIP screen, stretched her arm out in front of them, and placed her head on his shoulder, the hand with the Solo ring held up between them. 'Cheese!'

Julius wasn't quite sure about the quality of his own smile, but he gave it his best shot, considering the circumstances.

'There,' she said, closing the PIP. 'I've just sent it to you. Must treasure every moment.'

For the first time, Julius detected a hint of sadness in her voice, but it passed away as quickly as it had arrived.

'I must go now,' she said, standing up.

'Sure, me too. It was my friend's birthday yesterday, and we're having lunch together,' he said. 'Will I see you around?'

Farrah looked at him, almost as if she was studying his face. 'Why not? You have my number.' With that, she waved, and walked off.

Julius didn't move until a few minutes later; he was feeling slightly worried about the fact that his heart was still beating hard in his chest.

When he joined the others — in what turned out to be a Jamaican restaurant — it took all of his willpower to refrain from telling Skye and Faith how the meeting really went, because Morgana was there too. Even though she was going out with Maks, he still felt a little too uncomfortable to talk about Farrah in front of her, and maybe even a little guilty. The guys didn't need to know *everything* anyway, and particularly not about his gaping mouth or his out-of-control heartbeat, so he decided to play it cool and keep his thoughts about her to himself for a little longer.

CHAPTER 3

OUTER SPACE THRILLS

The next morning Julius was up and running rather early, which made Skye very suspicious. 'Are you OK?' he asked as Julius emerged from the bathroom, fully dressed and ready to go.

'For sure,' Julius replied, offhand. 'Why?'

'Because it's 8 o'clock *and* it's Sunday morning?'

'So?'

Skye brushed his fringe out of his eyes, and stared intently at Julius. 'There's something you're not telling me.'

'It's our first chance to try the Moonrising's holospheres! I don't want to queue forever. Do you?'

Skye didn't seem too convinced. 'Fine,' he said, and swung his legs over the side of the bed. 'Give me a moment.'

As soon as he had disappeared into the bathroom, Julius switched his PIP on and, leaning against the room's scenery screen – which was broadcasting sunrise over the ocean – he opened up the picture of Farrah, and let out a long sigh. There was something the matter with him all right, but he had no intention of admitting it. Deep down, he was even a little afraid that Skye would make a move on her, just because he was, well, Skye Miller.

Julius had spent the night thinking up all sorts of excuses for going to Satras, while avoiding sounding too desperate, and in the end he had settled on the games, which were *always* a good enough reason for the Skirts. As Skye got ready, Julius sent a message to Faith and Morgana, arranging for them to meet them in the mess hall at 08:30. Luckily, neither of them found the request strange and happily agreed to the plan.

When they reached the holofloor in New Satras, a familiar face waved at them from the information kiosk.

'Mrs Mayflower!' cried Morgana, running towards her. 'It's so good to see you!'

'Eeeeh! Look who's here,' said the old lady excitedly. 'My favourite team.'

'I didn't know you were coming along as well,' said Julius, noticing that her wrinkles had multiplied greatly, since the summer.

'There was nothing much left to do in Satras,' she explained. 'No customers, no fun. I'd rather be here, in the thick of it. Besides, I owe those Arneshians a lesson on how to treat old ladies!' she said, punching her left palm with her other fist.

'That's the spirit!' said Faith.

Julius grinned. True enough, she had almost been kidnapped two years before but, judging by her resolute attitude, she was definitely on good form. 'Well, we're glad you're here.'

'Thank you, my dearies,' she said, sounding genuinely moved. 'So, did you come to look at our facilities?'

'Yes,' answered Faith. 'What's the story on New Satras?'

'Very similar to home, really,' explained Mrs Mayflower. 'Only, there are far less holospheres and fewer games going on at any one time. They do it to save power, but also in case of emergency. Players need to be able to get out of their spheres quickly and you can't afford to have 300 people stuck in there at the same time if anything goes wrong.'

'Fair enough,' said Faith. 'Do you have a little space for us today?'

'Of course. Fight or Flight?'

'Flight!' cried Morgana. 'Everyone for themselves.'

'One Flight token coming up. Enjoy!'

'Julius?' called Skye. 'Are you coming or not?'

Julius, who was currently facing away from the booth for some reason, turned around, looking oddly surprised. 'Wha … oh! Yeah. I was just–'

'You're weird, you know that?' said Skye, dragging him into the changing rooms.

Julius had, of course, been distracted as he looked for Farrah, in the off chance she had decided to take a walk down there. Unfortunately, his focus didn't improve very much in the games and he ended up getting shot down so many times by everyone else that it was almost embarrassing.

'McCoy!' shouted Morgana, after destroying Julius for the tenth time in a row. 'What the heck was that? Do you even want to play?'

'Sorry guys,' he said, trying to sound like he was under the weather. 'I don't feel too well. I think I'll just wait for you outside. If I take another turn I'll probably throw up in my lap.'

'Good grief,' said Faith. 'That's never a good idea, as me grandma Allappa used to say, whenever someone threatened to throw up on themselves ... or their friends for that matter.'

Julius stared ahead blankly, pondering Faith's words for a moment, and then shook his head. 'I'll see you shortly.' He disconnected from the game and climbed out of his holosphere. He was feeling perfectly fine, but it was obvious that his mind was focused elsewhere, so he got changed and exited out into the courtyard, where he sat watching the rest of the Skirts' games on one of the large arena screens.

'I've seen you do a lot better than that.'

Julius turned and saw a Zed officer sitting at the top of the steps, holding a takeaway cup of coffee. He didn't recognise the man, but he had three pale blue stripes on each of the sleeves of his jacket and the Earth symbol against a grey shield: the symbol for all Curiates. Julius guessed that he must then have been at the docks, the year before, when Ambassador T'Rogon had landed on the Moon. The man had rather an official air about him, with his tightly cropped hair and pristine uniform. Julius stood and bowed, and watched as the man did the same.

'Ben Hastings,' he said, shaking Julius' hand. 'Do you mind if I sit with you for a while?'

'Not at all,' answered Julius, feeling quite intrigued and chuffed that he was being approached by such an important man.

'The Skirts are on top form today,' he said, pointing at the screen.

'Apart from me, obviously,' Julius added in a low-key manner.

'We all have our off days, you know.'

Hastings had a warm smile, which reminded Julius of Clavel's. Like the professor, he seemed to have an easy-going attitude. It was evident in his eyes, and by the many orange-coloured wisps which were floating around him. Those, in particular, put Julius at ease. 'I guess so. Do you play, sir?'

'Don't bother with the *sir*, please. We're just having a friendly chat,' he replied, amicably. 'I used to play but, since I joined the Curia, time has become a precious commodity for me. Not to mention this whole mess with the Arneshians.'

Julius nodded, understanding him all too well.

'Hey, I hope I didn't offend you before. I know very well what you can do, in case you're wondering.'

'It's OK. I can safely admit that I was pretty rubbish back there.'

'In the office we have bets on student teams, and I picked you guys from the start.'

'Really?'

'We need to have some R&R too, you know? Anyway, I just wanted to say that the Skirts are the best team we've seen on Satras for many, many years. And, if I may, you are the star of the team.'

'I wouldn't be without the others,' answered Julius, reddening slightly.

'Don't be modest, Julius,' said Ben, jovially. 'Your team is everything, I know. But you have been gifted beyond hope. Take pride in it, and use your gift to bring hope back to us. Be a White Child.'

Julius couldn't help but feel mightily pleased. To receive such a compliment from one of the Curiates was quite an honour.

Just then, the screen announced the end of the game, and Hastings stood up. 'I have to get back now. Don't tell Miller that I said you're the star, or he'll come storming into my office.'

'I won't,' said Julius, getting to his feet. 'I promise.'

'It was good meeting you finally.' And with that, he left.

It was a nice way to right the wrongs of a bad game and, as Julius waited for his friends, he imagined what it would have felt like if Farrah had been there next to him, listening with admiration to the Curiate's words. When the Skirts emerged from the changing rooms, they found him daydreaming on the steps, looking chuffed.

Much to his frustration however, Julius didn't manage to bump into Farrah that weekend so, when Monday arrived, as well as being distracted, he had also become a little touchy. Luckily, Professor Farshid had decided to take the students for a full tour of Moonrising; from the top of the ship to the bottom. That gave Julius a further chance to look for Farrah, both inside BM Sield, and in New Satras. He didn't spot her anywhere, but he felt better just for trying. It was only during Professor Clavel's class, that afternoon, that Julius' mind was able to focus properly on the task at hand.

'Mizkis,' said Clavel, 'given our re-location, it is time to introduce you to a new space vehicle.'

A few whispers broke out among the students.

'I know that some of you have had a chance already,' he said pointing at Morgana and Faith.'

'It's the sky-jet!' cried Skye, excitedly.

Clavel nodded, and that was enough to send the Mizkis into a frenzy.

'Finally!' said Julius, giving Faith a high-five.

'Here's how we're going to do it,' said Clavel, hushing them. 'Moonrising's current low speed will allow us to use the next couple of hours for some real practice; no simulation.'

Both Julius and Faith had to place their hands on Morgana's shoulders, to stop her from bouncing up and down in her seat.

'Our 5 and 6MSs will provide aerial support, while you're out there. In case of emergency, they will bring you back in. Follow me to the hangar now.'

Julius was really looking forward to this. It was hard to believe that, shortly, he would be out in space, far from his solar system, driving a sky-jet alongside a battleship. As he walked through the hangar with the other students, he tried to take in all the bits of advice that Faith and Morgana were sharing, learnt during their Summer Camp experience at Pete's. To Julius' surprise, he found out that Skye hadn't yet tried it out, despite the fact he had been raised on a space station. Due to age restrictions, he wasn't allowed, which was why he was now looking every bit excited as Julius.

In the hangars, Professor Clavel took them up a flight of stairs, to a mezzanine level. The ceiling was much lower here but, from the edges of the platform, there was a great view of the Cougars below.

For the first time, Julius was able to appreciate just how many machines there were onboard, and the sheer amount of engineers and mechanics, who were zooming busily between the aircrafts.

'Here we are,' said Clavel, pointing towards an area below and to the opposite side of the Cougars. 'Welcome to Sky-Jet Central.'

The Mizkis rushed to the banister and looked with amazement at the sea of space-scooters waiting there for them.

'Pick any one you like, from the front row, please,' Clavel instructed them.

Julius hurtled down the steps, three at a time, clearing the last four with one leap, while Faith hovered nonchalantly over his head. He stopped beside the first available one and walked around it, studying all of its parts. It looked very much like the everyday fly-scooters that could be bought back on Earth. The seat was long enough to take two people, and it ended in a high back that rose up above head-height. There was a gap for the legs, between the seat and the handlebars, with a small storage compartment underneath it. The jet was the colour of hard coal: a deep, murky grey that would blend perfectly with the dark expanses of space. The words, "BM Tijara" were etched into the front panel, above the emblem of Zed.

'Hop on, so I can show you the controls,' said Clavel.

Julius took his seat and was glad to find that it was soft and comfortable.

'Essentially, the sky-jet drives like a scooter,' explained Clavel. 'We use it to carry people outside a space station; to collect items and deliver them around the orbital space. They are never used for fighting though. To move forward, you rev the right throttle, and use the handbrakes to stop.

You can also reverse by pressing the red button on the left handle.'

Julius identified all of the mentioned parts, and found the reverse button on the left, which could be activated with a flick of the thumb.

'There's a menu on your central touch-screen. Activate it now, please.'

Julius did so, and it lit up in green. The words, "New User – Log in" flashed up briefly, before being replaced by an empty box and keyboard.

'Today, Mizkis,' said Clavel, 'you have the opportunity to create your tag-names, which will be used every time you participate in a mission.'

'I've dreamt of this day since I was a little girl ...' enthused Morgana. 'I still do!'

Skye glanced sideways at her. 'You need to get out more, woman. I'm gonna have a word with Maks, that's what I'll do.'

Morgana was far too mesmerised by the green screen to take any notice of him, and kept wringing her hands together.

Julius began to rack his brain for a name to use. It would have to be short and have a cool ring to it, he reckoned. 'I wish Clavel had given us the heads up for this,' he whispered to Faith, who simply nodded thoughtfully.

'Hey, why don't we choose a theme,' proposed Skye, 'as members of the Skirts?'

'Good idea,' said Faith. 'Like animals or metals, you mean?'

'Exactly,' answered Skye. 'What about birds?'

'I knew you'd say that ...' said Julius.

'I like it,' said Morgana. 'Can I be «Swan»?'

'Better you than me,' chirped Faith.

'I was thinking more along the lines of birds of prey, you know?' said Skye. 'Something a bit more ... ferocious than a swan.'

'You'll be a vulture then, Miller,' said Faith. 'On account of your eating habits.'

'Hey, I don't eat corpses,' he grumbled.

'That's because you haven't run out of food yet.'

Skye pondered the remark. 'Hmm ... You know what? I like it. I'll be Vulture.'

'Good man,' said Faith. 'I'll take Baza.'

'I'll be Goshawk,' said Julius.

'Nice one,' said Morgana. 'I'm going for Kite then.'

Julius typed his tag name into the box and pressed his thumb against the starting pad, to tie it to his personal profile. The name immediately flashed up on a small screen at the front of his jet.

Once all the Mizkis had picked their names, Clavel continued the lesson. 'From the menu, you can select your front light, send distress codes, open the intercom, and several other functions that we will explore as we go. Last, but not least, you will need to activate your cupolas. A cupola is the name of the protective field that allows you to be *out there* without a spacesuit. I want you to activate those now, and keep your feet inside the vehicle.'

Julius selected his, and the field sprung up, promptly cutting off all outside noise. He looked at the shimmering dome above his head and touched it cautiously; although it did have some give, it was still pretty solid. His screen blinked, asking him to open the inter-con.

A second after he did so, Clavel came on-air. 'You're now ready to go,' he said. 'Follow me outside, in single file, one after the other.'

Julius watched as Clavel hopped onto one of the sky-jets and fired up the machine. As its cupola appeared, its lights came on and it lifted off the floor.

'Engines on, Mizkis. You can talk to each other, by calling up the respective tag names on screen; you can select as many as you want at any one time. These machines have a fairly long range, but you may lose contact in certain areas of space. All right, let's move it.'

Julius turned the engine on; it made a whooshing noise as it came to life, which faded to a gentle rumble, reminding him of the power contained within the machine's turbines. As soon as Morgana started to move away, Julius edged his sky-jet forward behind her. It was extremely responsive, and he didn't need to give it too much power to make it go fast. He slowed down to the designated safety speed that all pilots were told to use within the hangar; he was already beginning to adjust well to the machine.

Clavel stopped and gathered the Mizkis together inside one of the airlocks; once the last student was safely sealed inside, he opened up the port door.

Julius was completely awestruck as he inched forward. This was different to the other times he had been outside, in the Stork and the various other transport vessels. In those, there had been ceilings and walls which felt quite reassuring, but in the sky-jet, the only thing separating him from the vastness of space was a thin shield. He realised that he was, in reality, just a little creature and was suddenly conscious of his own fragility. He could hear his heart beating fast in his chest, in the silence within his jet's cupola. Although the temperature had remained constant and warm, he shivered instinctively on seeing the dark emptiness around him.

He steadied himself and continued following Clavel, aware that a large number of Cougars had just left BM Tijara, and were slowly patrolling the surrounding space area.

His intercom crackled on, and Clavel spoke.

'You have about 90 minutes to get to know your jets. Try manoeuvres, different speeds, turns, and whatever else you want. We aren't going to have too much practice time after this, so you need to be really confident as soon as possible. Those of you with experience should help the others. Off you go!'

Julius began by turning his sky-jet around, so he could admire the full might of Moonrising as it towered before him. He wasn't able to actually take it all in at such close quarters, but he figured if he wanted to get a proper view of the ship in its entirety, he would probably need to stray quite far, something he was pretty sure they *weren't* allowed to do. He opened up a com-channel with the Skirts and, together, they began to try all sorts of drills involving twists, bends and mad chases. The sky-jets were fast and easy to pilot, which made the session incredibly varied. Every so often — or regularly in the case of Barth — a couple of Cougars had to intervene and round up the stragglers, any time they forgot to keep up with Moonrising, which was naturally moving forward on its set course. At the end of the lesson, the Mizkis were still having so much fun that it took Clavel another 20 minutes before he could get them all safely inside the airlock, and even that only happened after he had threatened to order the Cougars to open fire.

That evening, after dinner, the excitement still hadn't died down, so most of the 4MAs went to the lounge to write up their logs, exchange tips, and compare notes. After a couple of hours of intense conversations, Julius decided to get himself a hot chocolate and went over to the counter. As he waited for his drink, he opened his PIP to look at the picture Farrah had taken of them, which had now become quite a regular thing. He was so engrossed in this, that he didn't notice Skye walk up behind him.

'Gotcha!' he said, over his shoulder.

Julius closed his PIP abruptly, and his cheeks flushed red. 'Don't, Miller.'

'*Now* I understand what's been going on with you lately, you sly dog,' he said, with a cheeky wink.

Julius couldn't suppress a half-smile, but he still didn't want to encourage Skye's taunts, so he forced a straight face.

'Can we at least talk about it?' Skye asked him, simply. 'You're my best mate, Jules, so I'm not going to mess with you about this. Please?'

Julius grabbed his cup and moved to one of the empty tables, motioning for Skye to follow him. Once seated, he opened up the picture again and showed it to him.

Skye looked at it for a long time, then said, 'You're in serious trouble my friend. And any guy would *beg* to have such trouble.'

'Tell me about it,' said Julius. Gradually, he began to open up to Skye, and described their first meeting, and how he had felt when she had put her head on his shoulder, or touched his arm.

'Your smile looks a bit weird in that pic ... were you feeling ok? Anyway, she's stunning, man. And she kicked your butt at Solo. When's your next date? Or proper first date?'

'Date?' gulped Julius, panicking. 'No … we didn't arrange a date.'

'What? How did you leave things, when you parted ways? Did you tell her to have a nice life, or something? Please tell me you didn't!'

'No, actually. I asked her if I would see her around and all she said was, "Why not. You have my number." '

'Unbelievable,' said Skye, slapping his forehead. 'You've managed to memorise her last words, but you still don't have a date. Are you man or amoeba? Why haven't you called her? You don't need an excuse, you know?'

'I don't?'

'Do you?'

'Well, I thought that it would look less … pushy if I did.'

Skye put on his best affairs-of-the-heart face. 'What do you have to use as a reason for calling her? Let's have it.'

'Well, there's the Solo ring box, which I haven't given her yet.'

'Use it. Perfect excuse. Send her a message, right this instant. Tell her something like, apologies for not getting back sooner, but you had internal active duties that kept you up all night.'

'But that's not true,' protested Julius, feeling a bit like he was being swept up by a whirlwind.

'Silence! You've let more than 48 hours pass without making contact, and although a little waiting is healthy, too much can cheese a girl off, big time. Besides, active duties is one of those magic bunch of words that makes you look good, and competent.'

'It's two words, actually.'

'That's beside the point. So, as I was saying, you then ask her how she is and when it'll be convenient for her to meet up, so you can give her the box.'

'*Then* what?'

'Then the ball is in her court, and we wait. You can't plan everything, McCoy.'

Julius sighed and nodded, trying to remember all of Skye's recommendations for the message. 'Ok, thanks. But you *must* keep this to yourself, you understand me?'

'Count on it,' he replied. He stood up and was about to go rejoin the others, when he stopped and turned to Julius again. 'I've got to ask, man: what about Morgana?'

'What about her?' he answered, blankly.

'You know what I mean.'

'She made her choice, didn't she?'

Skye looked at him, 'I guess she did. You *both* did.'

That evening, after saying goodnight, Julius returned to his room, eager to put together his message for Farrah. It took him almost half an hour to write 10 lines, but he wanted to make absolutely sure he had included all of Skye's suggestions. Eventually, after re-reading it five times, he sent it, and drew a long breath. 'What will be, will be.'

The first thing Julius did the next morning was to check his PIP but, to his dismay, there was no reply from Farrah yet.

'She's probably still asleep,' said Skye, trying to sound convincing, while yawning.

Unfortunately, the story was the same every morning that week, right into the weekend, and the week after. By the time Sunday the 21st of October had come around, Julius had become truly miserable and Skye's excuses for Farrah's silence were running dry. He had even considered checking with Maks, but the thought of Morgana finding out was enough to put him off and encourage him to try come up with another plan.

It was around lunchtime of that day that people began to hear rumours about the mission. There was an increasingly common one that some of the Earthlings had been located at last, in the Delphinus constellation.

Julius, like everyone else on board, finally had something else to focus on, and even Farrah's reply — or rather lack thereof — was put to one side for the moment.

The Skirts, along with Siena, Isolde and Barth, were having lunch at the Jamaican restaurant, which had become quite popular with their group.

'I hate waiting,' said Skye, eating a double portion of goat curry. 'And I hate rumours.'

Julius was munching a chicken leg, lost in thought, when the "Breaking News" sign flashed up on the large TV screen at the far end of the restaurant.

'Look,' said Morgana. 'It's Mielowa. I didn't know she came with us.'

But there she was, Iryana Mielowa, the Space Channel's very own roving reporter, sporting a new auburn bob with a razor-sharp edged fringe, and a dark brown shade lipstick.

'Good afternoon, Moonrising,' she said, with a charming smile. 'The Space Channel has been officially authorised to report that some of our people have been located at last, in a nearby classified location.'

An excited buzz ran through the restaurant. Mielowa turned to her right, and the camera panned to include Aldobrando Roversi. Julius thought that he looked pretty much the same as he had last year, but perhaps with a touch more grey hair than before.

'I'm here with the Curio Maximus,' Mielowa continued, introducing her guest, 'to find out more about our recent discovery. Mr Roversi, what can you tell us about it?'

'We are extremely pleased with our progress, Ms Mielowa,' he said, confidently. 'It took us the best part of five months to track this location, but we have done it.'

'How was that achieved, Curio?' said Mielowa.

'Our enemies have left behind a particularly strong signature, which has allowed us to track them through space. Incidentally, the very technology they have used against us — from the static field that ground us to a halt, to the teleportation devices — have also been put to good use. Thanks to our brilliant technicians, we now know how to use them and we *will* use this knowledge to send our people back.'

'This is marvellous news, Curio,' said Mielowa, all smiles. 'Tell us, how have you been able to confirm where our people actually are? I understand that we're talking about a sizeable area on a small planet.'

'Given the circumstances,' said Roversi, affably, 'I can afford to disclose just a few more details. We tracked their signature all the way to their location, then used a sensor scan to detect that indeed there were bio-signatures present.

After that, we used their very own teleportation technology to relay a message into the midst of the group. We had to wait several days before someone took charge, worked out our instructions, and sent a reply. And there's more.'

'Yes?' said Mielowa, totally engrossed.

'The person who replied was none other than Mr Chris High, Voice of the Earth for Oceania.'

'No!' cried Mielowa, clasping her hands to her chest. 'Does this mean that …?'

'Exactly. Mr High has confirmed he is still in the company of the people who were in Oceania at the time of the abduction.'

'How many people are we talking about here?'

'20 million, give or take,' said Roversi.

Mielowa dabbed a finger to the side of her right eye, as if she was drying a little tear. Then she turned to the camera. 'You heard it here first. Iryana Mielowa, Space Channel.'

Raucous cheers erupted from every table in the restaurant. Even the passersby, who had stopped to watch the broadcast, were now clapping and chattering away in animated fashion.

'This is just!' cried Julius, waving the half-eaten chicken leg around, while Siena and Morgana tearfully embraced each other.

'We *have* to go find George and Felicity,' said Morgana, leaping up suddenly.

'Let's go,' agreed Siena. 'Later, guys!'

Julius knew why, and appreciated what a nice gesture it was from the girls. Their classmates George Lowet and Felicity Steep, were from Australia and New Zealand respectively, so they were bound to be emotionally involved in the rescue mission, more than anyone else in their class. On the down side, however, it seemed clear that they hadn't found Europe's former inhabitants yet. Julius looked up at Faith, and saw the same disappointed expression in his eyes.

'I guess we should be pleased for them,' was all he could muster.

'Sure. But I just want me family back.'

'Have the Arneshians split them up according to their continents, or something?' asked Skye, cleaning his plate with a healthy chunk of fresh bread.

'Maybe,' answered Julius, leaning back in his chair. '*20 million* though. How are we going to get them all back?

'It's going to take forever,' added Skye.

'Not necessarily,' said Faith. 'We have their teleportation technology now, and we know how to use it. What bothers me is how we actually found out about their location.'

'You heard the Curio,' said Skye. 'We followed the Taurus One's signature.'

Faith shook his head. 'That day, by the time we were able to move again, the Taurus One had gone to warp and if the Arneshians have two brain cells between them that work properly, they would have also used hyperjump a few times, just for good measure. On top of that, our people have been kept on that planet for six months, if not more, some 100 light years away.'

'So?' asked Julius, not liking where this was heading.

'*So*, there is no known device that can track and follow a ship's signature under those circumstances. If you ask me, the Curia had another lead, and they're just telling us a story to fill in the gaps.'

'But why?' asked Skye.

'I don't know. Maybe they want to keep some details classified, in case there's a spy on board — either human, or holo.'

'*On Moonrising*?' said Skye. 'It's practically Zed on holiday. There are no strangers on board. Surely, we would have noticed an intruder.'

'Mind you,' added Julius. 'They've been able to sneak Arneshians into Zed before, remember. I guess I don't mind them being a little cautious, if that's the case.'

There was no disagreeing with that, so they continued to discuss the impending rescue mission for the rest of the afternoon. When dinner time arrived, they remained where they were, ordered some more food and were joined by more of the 4MAs. Morgana also returned, accompanied by Maks. Soon enough, Julius found himself chatting to him, all the while trying hard to ignore his arm around Morgana's shoulder, which irritated him greatly. At the same time, he was still hoping to spot Farrah, among the crowd but, as curfew approached, he realised that yet another day had passed by with no word from her.

CHAPTER 4

ON THE USE OF POWER

After a typically exhausting session practicing with their shield implants, the 4MAs made their way to the mess hall, for a much deserved lunch.

Julius was limping slightly, as he recovered from a cramp in his left leg, thanks to Morales and Chan's intense training. 'I swear,' he said, massaging his sore calf. 'Those two were meant for each other.'

'And I thought Morales was nice,' added Skye. 'She's worse than him! Did you see the lack of pity on her face when I fell over in agony?'

'Yeah,' added Faith. 'But that's probably because it was the fourth time you were trying that stunt on her to get out of class.'

'So? It should have worked the first time,' said Skye, looking disappointed. 'I'm losing my touch with her.'

'Whatever you do,' added Morgana quickly, 'don't you go wearing that awful perfume again, please.'

'Nah,' he replied. 'I think it would be too late anyway. She's under his spell now. I see the way she looks at him. The man in black has won.'

'I bet it was his pointy goatee that did it,' said Morgana, nudging him in the ribs. 'He's more mature, and that's what a woman needs: a mature person by her side. Someone to rely on in dire straits.'

Julius was about to say something about Maks *not* being there for her when it mattered, but bit his lip.

'I could grow a goatee too,' said Skye, defensively, 'if I wanted too.'

'Yeah right,' she said, grinning. Then she screamed and ran on ahead, as Skye turned suddenly and began to tickle her.

'Baby face! Baby face!' she chanted, goading him and laughing all the while.

Faith seemed to enjoy the chase, while Julius' eyes were mainly focused on Skye's hands and their exact whereabouts as he proceeded to subdue Morgana. He knew they were only joking around, but why did he need to joke so blinking close to her body? And why was she giggling like that? And why–

His PIP suddenly vibrated, interrupting his thoughts. He looked down and froze on the spot; there was an incoming vidcall from Farrah. He swallowed, forgot about everything else and said, 'Go ahead guys, I'll catch up in a minute.'

Skye stopped in mid tickle, still holding onto Morgana, who was staring at him, and wondering what had happened. Skye's eyes met Julius' and it was clear that he had realised exactly what was distracting his friend. There wasn't any need for telepathic skills to figure that one out.

'We'll see you in the mess hall,' said Skye, dragging Morgana away, despite her protests.

'What's happening?' she asked, aware that something had passed between Julius and Skye.

'Never you mind, Miss "If-he's-not-old-as-my-grandpa-I-won't-date-him".'

Julius watched them walk away, while a hot flush ran over him. With a trembling finger, he pressed the onscreen button and opened the channel.

'Hi Julius!' she said, her lovely smile filling the screen.

Julius was once again taken aback by her beauty. Even though he hadn't seen her for almost three weeks, she was exactly like he remembered her, except she was perhaps looking a little tired, he thought. 'Hey Farrah,' he said, trying to sound as natural as possible. 'It's good to see you. I thought my message had gotten lost or something.'

'I'm so, so sorry, Julius,' she replied and, by all accounts, it looked like she really meant it. 'I only saw it this morning.'

'Oh. Was your PIP down or something?'

'They shut it down ... I was in hospital again.'

Realising now that the reason she hadn't replied had nothing to do with him made him feel incredibly relieved. 'Are you ok now?'

'Back to normal, I guess,' she said, shrugging her shoulders.

'If I'd known I would have come visit you.'

'You're sweet. I wish you had known ... I would have liked that very much,' she said, lowering her eyes.

Julius was vaguely aware that his cheeks were becoming pretty warm, and surely turning a dark shade of red, but quite frankly he didn't seem to care that much. The open way she was talking to him, as if they had known each other for more than just three weeks, made him feel completely at ease and more eager to see her than ever before. 'I've been carrying the box with me ever since I wrote you. Do you think we could meet? I mean, if it's ok with you.'

'Are you kidding?' she laughed. 'I'd love to see you again!'

Julius tried hard, and quickly realised that he couldn't really find a suitable reply to that.

His oversized smile must have done the trick, however, because she nodded happily and said, 'Great! Why don't you meet me by my parents' shop, on Saturday afternoon, at 2 o'clock? It's called Auld Oddities.'

'It's a da– a ... plan, I mean. Yeah, great. Yeah.' At that point he made the decision to hang up before he could embarrass himself. 'Till Saturday, then.'

'Till then,' she said.

The moment he stepped inside the mess hall, he knew he wasn't going to be able to hide the elation he felt swelling in his chest. It was written all over his face, which was why Skye just nodded, as he came to meet him at the door, and gave him a congratulatory double pat on the shoulder. 'Saturday afternoon,' was all Julius could say.

'Nice work, McCoy. Hey, listen,' said Skye, as they walked back to the others, 'Morgana was nagging me about what was going on, and Faith was getting pretty curious too. All I said is that it was this Solo girl you'd met, and you needed to give her the box back.'

Julius thought about it for a moment. 'It's fine, don't worry. In fact, it's probably easier if they know.'

'Besides Julius, who did you think you would fool with *that* grin?' he added, cheekily. 'You could see it from Earth.'

When they got to the table, Morgana simply waved at him and continued her conversation with Siena. If she was pretending not to be interested, she was doing a pretty good job of it, thought Julius. Faith, on the other hand, wanted to be brought up to scratch, while Skye was anxious to find out what they had said to each other. It made for a rather intense lunch chat, or, in Julius' case, just chat, since he was so absorbed by recounting and revisiting their call, that food was the *last* thing on his mind.

Talking to Farrah had had the effect of a month's worth of gene therapy on Julius, whose powers peaked superbly that afternoon, to the astonishment of both Professors King, and Beloi.

For their telekinesis lesson, King had created an obstacle course in the cargo bay, and asked the students to pair up. Julius ended up with Faith, and his job was to levitate and manoeuvre him past each obstacle, without letting him drop to the floor. His powers were so heightened, that not only did he literally zoom Faith from A to B in record time, but he then proceeded to fire him back to A, then back to B, then A, and so on and so forth, faster and faster, until eventually Faith put a stop to it by throwing up indecently all over the floor.

When he arrived in Beloi's class for their last hour of lesson, Julius finished his day with a superior display of telepathic skills. The famous mirror labyrinth, in which they had been practicing since second year, had been reassembled on Moonrising, and Professor Beloi had gone the extra mile to make it as challenging as their present mission called for. When Beloi asked them to find a partner, Faith refused point blank to work with Julius, which forced a nervous Skye to take his place.

They were told to guide their partners around, and out of, the maze; only, this time, they wouldn't just be hindered by scramblers, but also by Arneshian holos, which the Mizkis had to fight off their path. Julius whisked Skye through the labyrinth, destroying all obstacles for him, and a few of his classmates' opponents too, just for good measure. The scramblers didn't even begin to bother him, his thoughts were so loud and clear that they were heard by all the students in the labyrinth, preventing them from hearing their own guides. Surprisingly, Professor Beloi seemed quite amused by this, and urged the other students to try and block Julius' voice from their minds. Unfortunately, no one was able to do so and, at the end of the hour, all of his classmates, bar Skye, were still stuck in the labyrinth being chased by holos.

'*McCoy*,' said Beloi, before Julius could leave at the end of the lesson. '*Who is this pretty blonde girl, called Farrah*?'

Julius did a double take and was mighty relieved that Beloi spoke only telepathically, so no one else had heard him. *'She's a friend of mine, Sir. How do you know about her?'*

'She's all over your brain. Quite hard to miss,' said Beloi. *'I would recommend you see her before every mission: she makes a hell of a fighter out of you.'*

Julius couldn't agree more, and made a mental note to tell her that on Saturday. That is, if he could resist for another three days.

He checked the time and saw that he had more than two hours to go before curfew. After a quick shower, instead of heading back to the lounge, he made a run for the lifts and headed down to New Satras. He was intent on finding out exactly where Farrah's parents' shop was, so he wouldn't be late on Saturday. He looked at the floor chart near the entrance, and scanned the list of businesses on level -2. 'Auld Oddities,' read Julius, when he spotted it. 'Right above Rowan Square.' That was a start. He took the escalator to the right level, trying to think up a convincing excuse, in case he actually bumped into her. Fortunately, the floor was quite busy that afternoon, and Julius found it easy to move around without drawing too much attention to himself.

As he approached the shop, he slowed down and cautiously peered through the glass window. There was a tall lady behind the counter, probably Mrs Hendricks, wrapping something for a Tuala student. Julius studied her for a while, but failed to see any resemblance to Farrah, except perhaps for the wavy hair. 'Maybe she takes after her dad,' he thought.

He took a good look at the strange and unusual objects on the shelves, and realised that it was an antique shop. Some of the gadgets were completely unfamiliar to Julius, but some he recognised quite easily. There were music playing devices, phones of various sizes, and clocks; there was also a range of mirrors, number plates and jewellery. He would have liked very much to browse the place properly, but he was too afraid that Farrah might walk in. Perhaps on Saturday he would get a chance.

Unsure of what to do next, he headed towards a small cafe across the road from the shop. As he was about to enter, he saw Ben Hastings, sipping coffee at one of the tables. The Curiate was talking to someone on his PIP but, when he saw Julius, he smiled and motioned for him to come closer and have a seat.

Julius figured that talking to Ben was the perfect excuse for waiting around a while longer, on the off chance Farrah showed up, so he sat down gratefully.

'Of course, Aldobrando,' said Ben, into his mouthpiece. 'I'll join you in a short while ... Very well ... I'll take care of it.'

'Hello, Mr Hastings,' greeted Julius. 'How's the Curio Maximus?'

'Good of you to join me,' he replied, affably. 'The Curio is well. I'll tell him you asked after him. So, what brings you here tonight?'

'Och, just taking a walk,' said Julius, innocently. 'It's been a long day at school.'

Ben nodded. 'Busy at work too. I hate this war,' he said. 'I hate the Arneshians.'

Julius was surprised to hear a Zed official express his opinion so openly but, at the same time, he found it quite refreshing as well.

'If only Marcus had never fallen for Clodagh, we wouldn't be in this mess. Women ... The moment she stepped out of line, with her dreams of world domination, he should have neutralised her, right there and then. But he didn't, and he died because of it.'

Julius knew all about that particular tragic love story, although how exactly Marcus had died was not quite so well known.

'She was very clever,' continued Ben, 'I'll grant you that, but no mind-skills. And what is a person without powers? I'm sorry if I seem harsh to you, but that's what I believe.'

Julius wasn't quite sure how to reply. He sensed that Ben had just needed to let off some steam, rather than have a proper conversation about the issue, so he decided not to challenge him on anything he had said. One thing, however, he *did* feel the need to say. 'My brother is a Nuarn.'

'I know, Julius. So was mine,' he replied. 'There's very little I don't know, in my line of work, especially when it concerns you.'

Julius wasn't really shocked by that, even though he knew this was how Zed worked, and that there weren't many secrets in this particular family. 'Did your brother also join T'Rogon?'

'No. He died a few years back.'

'I'm sorry,' said Julius. 'Do you ever wonder what he would have done in my brother's place?'

'I think he would have gone too, or at least, that's what *I* would have done.'

That really caught Julius' attention, and he sat up straight in his chair.

'What choice did he have, anyway? Without mind-skills, he would have been at the mercy of others — a kind mercy perhaps, but still at their mercy. And what if he had decided to be loyal to his family and stay behind? He would have been kidnapped along with the others, and been at the mercy of *someone else*. Would you have liked that?'

'No,' said Julius, quickly. 'Not at all.'

'Neither would he, I imagine. He made his choice, according to his powers and talents, in the same way as you've made your choices, according to your powers. Never feel guilty about your mind-skills, because there's a reason for everything in this world. Michael wasn't meant to have them, but you were. At least that's what I believe.' He finished the last sip of his coffee, and stood up. 'I'm off to dinner with the Curiates, tonight. What about you?'

'I'll head back too,' answered Julius. 'Curfew soon.'

'Good talking to you again, Julius. See you around.'

Julius bowed and watched him disappear into the crowd. It was strange hearing it from someone else, but he agreed with what Ben had said about his powers. The thought that he could have been born normal had always bothered Julius, and he had grown up fully aware of just how special his life was, even without the whole White Child business.

As they headed to their Martial Arts class, on Wednesday afternoon, the 4MAs were surprised to find Professor Clavel, instead of Chan, waiting for them.

'What's going on?' asked Faith.

None of their classmates seem to know either, so they sat down in front of the teacher, and waited to be clued in. Julius noticed how tense Clavel looked — he could see it in his aura, which was stricken with red wisps.

'Mizkis,' he began, 'from this moment forward, you are on official duties, and all lessons are suspended.'

Julius turned to the others, wide eyed. It seemed the moment had finally arrived.

'I'm here to brief you on Operation Oceania, so please open your PIPs now.'

The class promptly followed his instruction.

'I'm downloading the schematics of the area where our people are being held. It has been decided that all Mizkis from 4th year up, will be flying the Cougars, together with our Zed fighters.'

Morgana looked at Julius, excitement all over her face.

'As students, you will be required to provide aerial support to our Storks, Herons and, most important of all, to our portals, which we will be using to teleport people back to Earth. And you will *not* land on that planet, or engage the enemy without permission. Understood?'

'Sir, yes Sir,' cried the students.

'We have divided the airspace into sectors. Each one of you will be assigned one, and there you will remain for the entire duration of the mission, or until you are personally recalled back to Moonrising. Each sector has a number of portals and aircrafts to protect. You will be told who your charge is in due course.'

'Sir,' said Isolde, 'when do we start?'

'Soon, Miss Frey. Before this weekend is over, we will get our people back.'

The Mizkis cheered at that, and several of them moved over to George and Felicity, and patted them on their backs in a show of support.

Clavel let the class calm down before continuing. 'Let's take a look at this place then.' He pressed a few buttons on the wall, and ten touch-table tops emerged from the floor, dotted all around the room. 'Group up around a table.'

Julius, Faith, Skye and Morgana headed for the nearest one.

'I wonder if they'll keep our class in the same sector,' said Skye.

'I hope so, guys,' said Morgana. She activated their table top, and a large blueprint popped into view.

Julius studied it and quickly realised that it was a massive facility with multiple areas, extending over many miles. 'And that's only the ground floor,' he said, feeling slightly disheartened.

'This can't be right,' said Skye, pressing the "depth" button. 'It says that there are *twenty* underground levels.'

'It means each one is large enough to contain roughly 1 million people,' said Morgana.

'If they've kept our people split into continents, like we think,' said Faith, 'just how big will the other rescue missions be?'

'The remaining continents have between 500, and 900, million people each,' said Julius. 'That is, if they've kept the Americas as one.'

'It'll take us *forever*,' said Skye.

'Guys, let's just focus on this one first,' said Morgana, being practical. 'I'm sure they'll find a way of doing things quickly, if they can.'

Julius nodded, knowing that she was right. He looked at the respective airspace areas and carefully studied each sector; there were also several pictures of teleportation gates, which he studied thoroughly.

Clavel walked around the room, stopping by each of the tables, and answering any questions. Eventually, he made it to the Skirts. 'How does it look?'

'Busy like an anthill,' answered Faith.

'You'd better not crash into each other, then,' said Clavel.

'Sir,' said Julius, 'are we expecting any hostiles?'

The others looked up at Clavel, with worried expressions.

'I would say so,' he replied, simply.

Julius nodded. 'We'll fight back, then.'

'We may have to, yes,' agreed Clavel. 'We are deploying the Mizkis to border patrol, to ensure that none of the Arneshian ships come close to Moonrising. It's a big task, but you will at least have a safe harbour behind you, in case of emergency.'

'Will we fly together, sir?' asked Morgana, pointing at the Skirts.

'I don't see why not, Miss Ruthier,' said Clavel. 'But it's not a time for bravado, understood?'

'Us?' said Faith, pretending to be mildly offended. 'Would we ever?'

Clavel looked at him, with one raised eyebrow, then moved forward to the next table.

Julius turned to the others and grinned, trying to look relaxed. But, deep down, he felt a rush of nervous adrenaline coursing through him. After all, combat often brought with it casualties.

As it turned out, Faith got a chance to prove Clavel right the day after. All Mizkis had been asked to check their Cougars, to ensure that they were ready to go at a moment's notice.

Faith, being Faith, had spent the whole day maintaining his aircraft, as well as those of his classmates. The 4MAs trusted him so much that, even if a qualified Zed engineer had deemed their Cougars fit to fly, they still wanted to hear it from Faith too. Siena seemed to be finding the oddest little noises coming from her plane, which left him having to check her engines at least twice every hour — not that he was complaining much about it, of course.

Around dinnertime, most of the students had left the hangar, leaving only Julius and Faith behind.

'Come on, Irish!' said Julius, impatiently. 'It's eight o'clock and I'm *really* hungry.'

'Almost there,' said Faith, hovering high above, his head buried inside one of the engines. 'I just need to tighten that pressure gauge ... over there ... nasty thing ...'

Julius sighed and, crossing his arms, he slumped to the floor and leaned back wearily against a tool trolley. A few minutes passed by, and he felt his head lolling forward, as it grew heavy.

'That guy is so weird.'

Julius' sat up quickly, startled awake by the sound of a boy's voice from behind him.

'I know, right?' said another one. 'How's *he* gonna fight?'

'He can't really. They keep him around as a handyman.'

'I can't stand the Skirts. Just because they win a bunch of games, they think they can do whatever they want.'

Julius realised they hadn't seen him sitting there, and decided that was probably a good thing. As long as Faith kept his head in the engine, he wouldn't even notice them, and he could just let them pass by. Knowing Faith, he figured, if he could avoid a confrontation, it would be for the best.

'That McCoy is the worst of the lot,' said the first boy. 'He wouldn't admit it last year, but that team selection for the challenge was rigged.'

That was when Julius recognised the voice: it was the blonde boy who had accused him of favouritism when he had chosen the team for the game against the Arneshians.

'Nah. The worst one is that cripple over there, if you ask me,' added his friend.

Hearing them use the word "cripple" acted like a wakeup call, because both Faith and Julius, straightened up at the same time and faced the two boys.

'Who are you calling a *cripple*?' asked Faith, flatly.

Julius looked at their uniform tags, and saw that they were both 5MSs. The blond boy's name was Sheldon Luner, and his big-mouthed friend was Ernie Dillon. Julius' first instinct was to give them a piece of his mind-skills, but thought better of it, while Faith, whose judgment was probably affected by the long, tiring day of work, flew directly at them, charging like a bull.

Julius had to duck as his friend passed over his head, at the same time trying to grab him by the skirt. Unfortunately, he barely brushed the edges of it, allowing Faith to park his fists in the middle of each of the seniors' faces. There was a loud *crunch*, which Julius recognised as the unmistakable sound of a nose being broken.

'By dose ...' cried Ernie Dillon, in agony. 'You broge by dose!'

Julius saw blood trickling through Ernie's fingers, as he clutched his hands to his face. Sheldon Luner, meanwhile, was lying flat on the floor, out cold, with Faith hovering in mid-air above him, breathing heavily. Julius could almost see the steam coming out of his nostrils, while his clenched fists had turned red from the impact, and Dillon's blood. In four years of friendship, Julius had never seen Faith lose his temper like that. Not even Adrian Sewell had been able to get him so upset; then again, that had been a long time ago, and Faith was a very different person now. He wasn't sure what he should do, but the arrival of an angry-looking Captain Foster resolved the problem for all of them.

Julius, Faith, Sheldon and Ernie were standing in Foster's office, while the Captain laid into them like there was no tomorrow. Faith wasn't uttering a single word, still visibly furious, so Julius volunteered to explain what had set his friend off.

Foster turned dangerously scarlet, and seemed shocked, appalled and flustered all at once. 'In forty years of service I have NEVER witnessed such behaviour between students! *Especially* students from the same school! How can we fight the Arneshians if we don't have a united front inside our own house?'

Julius just kept looking straight ahead, wondering what on earth was he doing there, since he hadn't actually done anything wrong.

'Luner, Dillon,' cried Foster. 'You will be referred to Master Cress for your idiocy. Shanigan, you and McCoy will put your hands to better use by cleaning the storage cupboard until midnight. And no dinner until then!'

'But, sir,' started Julius, 'what have *I* done?'

'You weren't quick enough to stop your friend from descending to animal level. What kind of a White Child are you, if you can't even use Stasis on a person!'

'What's Stasis?' said Julius, feeling crushed by the unfairness of all this.

'Sir,' whispered Luner, sheepishly, 'we do Stasis in fifth year.'

'So?' growled Foster.

'They're in *fourth* year.'

Foster seemed taken aback. Then he looked at Julius, unabashed, and resumed the shouting. 'What kind of a White Child are you if you can't even use *Telekinesis* on a person?'

Julius didn't even bother to reply at that point since, quite clearly, Foster was bent on giving him a punishment.

Twenty minutes later, Julius and Faith were cleaning dusty shelves in a cramped little room, just off the training sector of Tijara. It was a storage area for microchips, which had been boxed back on Zed, and were now needing unpacking.

Julius wiped down one of the bottom shelves, opened a box, and took out a stack of the chips. He began to place them upright against the back wall, without any specific order. He raised an eyebrow when he noticed a strange title, "Tijara's Ultimate Sacrifice" above an odd-looking logo, but he was too annoyed to think about it properly, and dismissed it as just another documentary about the death of Marcus Tijara.

It took Faith a long time, but eventually he broke the silence. 'Sorry, mate.'

Julius looked up, with a stack of containers in his hands, and shrugged his shoulders. 'Don't worry about it.'

'You shouldn't be here,' he replied. 'You had nothing to do with it.'

Julius knew that well enough but, frankly, he was more concerned with the seriousness in Faith's voice than the lack of food. 'I just didn't see it coming is all,' said Julius. 'You're the one that usually shrugs people like that off, not take them on.'

Faith hovered upwards, carrying a box. 'I spent five years of me life being laughed at because of me chair. Always last, always left out of every damn game or trip. People don't need to call you a cripple to make you feel like one.' He paused for a moment, unpacking a few of the items onto a higher shelf. 'When I came here I knew it would be different, and I said to meself that no one would ever treat me like that again. Dillon and Luner are just more of the Somers of this world, cowardly bullies, but I didn't expect to find any of them here, on Zed.'

'People are people, no matter where you are,' said Julius. 'I think we *are* lucky here, though. Douchebags like them are few and far between.'

Faith nodded. 'If I feel down, I can go to the Hologram Palace and get a room where I can ... walk again, and be just like you. But, outside I have to survive and fend for meself. That's why I shrug them off, like you said. I try to find some sort of inner strength, and it works most of the time.'

'Except tonight,' said Julius.

'Yeah, except tonight. Tonight me legs have been more useless than usual.' He paused for a second, as if mustering his courage. 'I was seven, you know.'

Julius stopped what he was doing, realising that Faith was about to tell him exactly what had happened to him.

'Me parents had gone to the house next door, leaving me little cousin Patty and I at home. She went outside, chasing after a ball. I was right behind her, so when she got in the middle of the road and that fly-car showed up at top speed, I knew what would happen. Me powers weren't strong enough to push her out of the way — heck, I didn't even know what powers I had back then — so I did the only thing I *could* do. I ran to her, shoved her off the road, and got hit in her place. It happened so fast …' Faith shook his head. 'And the thing is, *she's* me inner strength. Whenever I feel down in the dumps because I can't walk, I think of her. If I had to choose all over again, between saving Patty's life, or not being able to walk, I'd never hesitate — I would *always* choose her over me. We all have responsibilities. She was mine.'

Julius was left speechless, and all he could do was place a reassuring hand on the bottom of his skirt. 'You're a good guy, Faith.'

That night, as Julius lay in his bed, he couldn't help but think about Faith's words. He had done what he had because it was his duty, and he never questioned it, no matter what the consequences. Ben Hastings had told him that a person without powers was destined to a shallow existence, but was it true? Faith had lost a most precious gift, the freedom to walk and run, and yet, his life was richer than that of many people he had met. In his place, he may well have at least blamed his parents for leaving him alone at such a young age, with an even younger kid to look after, or the driver of the fly-car for being so reckless. But not Faith. His sense of responsibility and his inner strength kept him going, and he was braver even than Julius. How would he have coped without his powers? And never mind his legs because, in his mind he agreed with Ben, his skills were the most important thing there was.

CHAPTER 5

OCEANIA

Julius spent the next couple of days in a state of anxiety, fuelled by the impending mission and, of course, his meeting with Farrah. He wasn't the only one however, to feel the strain, and a sense of calm before the storm had permeated throughout Moonrising. Since the interview with Roversi, Iryana Mielowa had embarked on a live marathon of minute-by-minute updates on the situation, seemingly sleeping only a mere four hours per night. Yet, she always looked impeccable, which drew amazed comments from the female students, who were not looking quite so refreshed by the long wait.

The 4MAs had eventually been assigned to Sector 7, and divided into 6 groups — the Skirts, plus Isolde, had been named as the fourth toon. With them was a mixture of 5 and 6MSs from Tijara, alongside several Zed officers, all responsible for the defence of their zone. Julius had also discovered that Captain Kelly and the Ahura Mazda would be working much closer to the planet; knowing that Kelly was around made him feel much more confident.

On Saturday morning, the 4MAs had officially been told that they would be the armed escort for the Storks, their size being smaller and so more appropriate to their rank as apprentices. After a hurried lunch, Julius couldn't take the wait any longer and decided to head to New Satras, taking Skye along for moral support. He could feel a tight knot in the pit of his stomach as he arrived at level -2. Unconsciously, he kept flattening his hair, in between drying his palms on the sides of his trousers, and straightening his uniform.

'I'm going to head to that cafe over there, all right?' said Skye. 'Keep calm and you'll be fine.'

Julius nodded. He took the box out of his leg pocket and removed a bit of fluff which was stuck in one of the corners. Composing himself, he began to walk determinedly towards Auld Oddities. Just as he had reached the centre of the square, a loud siren exploded to life, followed by an announcement: 'All Mizkis and Zed officers report for duty immediately!'

Julius stopped dead in his tracks. 'Damn,' he cried. Suddenly, all the colours and decor began to fade around him, like fresh paint being washed away by rain, as Moonrising entered into battle mode. He turned around, looking for Skye and saw that he was running towards him.

'She's there!' shouted Skye, over the noise, pointing at the shop. 'Let's go!'

Julius looked, and felt a rush of blood flooding his face, as he spotted Farrah hurriedly closing her parents' shop door behind her. 'Farrah!' he called, heading towards her.

She heard his voice and, when she saw him, she waved in his direction.

As they met, Julius was sorely tempted to throw his arms around her, but thought better of it, so he stopped short of bumping into her and put one hand on her arm instead.

'Right on time,' she said. 'I thought I'd *never* see that box!'

'Come on,' said Julius, grinning, 'we'll talk on the way.' As he turned and began to power-walk, his hand slid down her arm; when he found her hand, he grabbed it, and was relieved to feel her locking her fingers between his. His heart skipped a beat. 'Uh ... this is Skye, by the way.'

'Hi there,' said Skye, shoving a few people out of the way, as they headed for the lifts. 'I've heard *so* much about you, and such a description that I had started to believe you didn't exist!'

Farrah smiled, blushing slightly as she threw a glance at Julius. 'Nice to meet you, Skye.'

'When he told me that he had stumbled upon the most beautif– ouch!' he yelped, as Julius' elbow shot into his ribcage. 'Never mind …' he whispered, feebly.

Farrah looked at the pair of them, and giggled. 'I need to take the lift at the far end. It's quicker for me.'

They took the stairs at a run, and came to a stop when they reached the transporter for Tijara. Even with the confusion all around, Julius still took note of how perfectly Farrah's olive-green uniform suited her hair colour and skin complexion.

'We should go out for a meal, all together,' said Skye, waving to her as he held the lift door open.

'Sounds great,' she replied, and then to Julius, 'Thanks for the box.'

He didn't want to let go of her hand, but he had no choice. 'Hey,' he said, moving closer to her. If his heart had been skipping beats before, it was now pounding furiously, as her face drew nearer. 'Be careful out there, all right? Cause I *really* would like to see you again.'

Before Julius could say anything else, she placed a light kiss on his cheek. 'Likewise,' she answered. With that, she turned and ran to her lift.

Skye had to drag Julius inside, as he was still rooted to the spot, turning a healthy beetroot colour.

'You'd better clean that lip balm off!' he said, grinning cheekily.

'No way. It'll be my lucky charm for today.'

When they reached the hangar, Faith, Morgana and Isolde were already there, waiting by the Cougars. The siren was still blaring, but, by now, it had become background noise.

As Julius and Skye joined their group, Clavel approached them. 'Who's in charge of Toon 4?'

All faces turned to Julius.

'McCoy, get your guys ready to go in five,' said Clavel, moving quickly to the next group.

Julius nodded, and faced the others. Solemnly, he put his hand forward, palm down. 'We will bring them back,' he said.

'So let it be!' they replied, as one, and placed their hands on top of Julius'.

They held there together for a moment. Julius could see red wisps pouring from their auras. 'Channel your fear and make it work for you,' he said. 'Failure is not an option. Let's go.' He watched as they all boarded their planes, throwing a last glance at Morgana. No matter what was going on elsewhere, he would always care for her, whether she knew it or not.

He climbed inside his Cougar, and placed his thumb on the recognition plate. As he did so, his tag name appeared in bright, yellow letters on both side-displays of the craft. 'Goshawk, ready to roll,' he said. When he looked at Isolde's plane, he saw that she had chosen "Ruby", as her tag name. He quickly created a channel for his toon, and one for the Zed officers, knowing that any communication from Moonrising would come through whether or not there was a free channel. He then opened a tab with all of his toon's vitals, and the state of their Cougars, which appeared as vertical red lines; he hoped he wouldn't have need to check that too often. 'Toon 4, this is Goshawk. Ready check and standby.' Immediately, the red lines turned green, one by one, giving Julius the go-ahead. 'Moonrising, this is Toon 4. We're ready to go.'

'Initiating departure procedure, Toon 4. Hunt hard,' a voice replied from the bridge.

Julius touched the tips of his right fingers to the smear of lip balm that Farrah had left on his cheek. A fresh whiff of cocoa wafted up to his nostrils, which immediately made him think of sand, sea, and sun cream lotion. He was so electrified by the memory of his encounters with Farrah that, right then, he felt like he could have stormed the planet all by himself. He was still buzzing about the fact that she hadn't let go of his hand *and* agreed to go out for dinner. He couldn't let those good signs go to waste; but, first, they had a continent to rescue. He switched on his engine and rolled onto the short runway, followed by his toon.

The outer airlock ports were all open; a thin membrane, similar to the Zed shield, protected the inner hangar from outer space, preventing the deck from depressurizing. The Cougars, however, could just fly straight through it to get out, or get back in.

Julius took hold of the ship's catalysts, and willed his Cougar forward. Immediately, it accelerated and broke through the membrane, out into space.

'It's rush hour, people,' said Faith, as the rest of the toon joined him outside Moonrising.

Julius looked up, through the transparent roof of his plane, and watched several layers of black Cougars positioning themselves in their own respective zones. Julius knew, somewhere among them, was Farrah; he wished now that he had asked her what sector she would be working in, or even what her tag name was. He touched his screen, bringing up the coordinates for Sector 7, and led his toon towards it. He could see his classmates' Cougars heading in his general direction, all flying together in tight formations. As they moved further away from Moonrising, groups of the planes detached and veered off to their posts, where Zed officers were already patrolling.

As he approached his zone, Julius spotted a teleportation gate. 'Look, guys!' he said. 'It's our portal.'

'Wow,' said Isolde. 'Will it really work?'

'I know, right?' said Morgana. 'I never even thought it would be possible.'

'It's slightly scary, if you ask me,' said Skye. 'How do you know you won't just end up ... *dispersing* yourself in the course of the journey?'

'It worked well enough for the Arneshians,' answered Faith. 'We only have to hope that List has properly recreated it.'

'What do you mean?' said Skye, in alarm. 'Hasn't this thing been tested yet?'

'It'll be fine, mate,' said Faith. 'I'm sure they've done homework aplenty before risking sending 20 million people through it.'

Skye didn't reply, but Julius understood his nervousness well enough, because he had also had the same concerns. This was, after all, a first for humans — or at least the non-Arneshian portion of mankind — and, although Zed had already been testing it for a few months, there was still no guarantee that all would go smoothly. Plus, there was the fact that it wouldn't just be *one* portal, but a series of them, as each carrier was taken back to Earth, quadrant by quadrant. Yes, thought Julius, there was reason for concern all right.

The portal was a massive 8 shaped structure, with each of the two circles functioning as a one-directional access path to and from Zed. Its silver metal frame shone bright in the darkness of space; tiny green lights marked the way in, while red ones dotted the way out. Julius guessed that, to get back home, the Storks would need to pick the green ones.

'Baza, Ruby,' said Julius, hailing Faith and Isolde. 'Keep your eyes on the planet, and alert us when the Storks begin to arrive.'

'Aye, aye, captain,' replied Isolde, veering her Cougar towards the edge of their zone, as close to the planet's airspace as they were allowed to go.

'Kite and Vulture,' called Julius again, 'you're with me on sector patrol. Make sure no one sneaks in from the shadows.'

'On it, Goshawk,' replied Morgana, promptly.

Julius steered his plane in the opposite direction and began to circle around the portal. Occasionally, he came across one of the seniors, who just nodded in his direction, before moving on. Julius could read all sorts of mixed emotions in their eyes, from fear to anxiety, not to mention the ashen-grey wisps swirling about in many of their cockpits. Only the auras of the Zed officers were mainly green, a clear sign of excitement, which was most likely thanks to their many years of training and experience. It was certainly good to have them around.

'Guys,' called Faith, after a while, 'I think they've started.'

Julius brought his plane about and zoomed in on the planet, using his scanner. There were so many planes above the rescue area that it was difficult to tell exactly what was going on. Then he noticed the Ahura, which was firing over a side section of the camp, where a large grey building stood. It was surrounded by barren land, which stretched for several thousand yards.

'Why are they shooting?' asked Isolde.

'According to Mielowa,' explained Faith, 'they're creating openings to let our ships go through.'

'Mielowa?' said everyone else, at the same time.

'Yes? She's on the radio doing a live report,' said Faith, defensively. 'At least I know what's going on.'

'Channel, please?' said Morgana.

'Well,' answered Faith, evasively, 'technically you don't have that kind of radio on a Cougar ...'

'But ... *you* do?'

'Just a little modification. You know me.'

'Yes, we know you, Baza,' said Julius. 'Keep us in the loop, then.'

'With pleasure,' replied Faith.

Julius shook his head, and wondered what else could be installed on a Cougar, if left in Faith's hands for long enough.

With the updates starting to come in fast from Faith, Julius resumed his patrol towards the furthest part of the sector, making sure to scan ahead for any unwanted visitors.

'They've just ceased firing on the camp,' said Faith. 'The Ahura Mazda has landed, together with the rest of the infantry party. They're going in!'

Julius took a deep breath, and stretched his hands, cracking his knuckles one by one, to ease the mounting tension. A sense of unease had drifted through his area, further heightening the sense of anticipation, and seemingly dragging time to a standstill.

'The transporters are now getting ready to land,' said Faith. 'There are thousands of them all lined up … but there's some resistance … wait …'

'What's happening, Faith?' implored Skye.

'There's some fighting going on.'

'Oh no,' said Morgana, sounding suitably worried.

'Faith?' urged Julius.

'Hold on,' he said. 'They won't allow our ships to land until the coast is clear. The combat troops have met the Arneshian guards, it seems.'

Julius was getting restless now. There was a battle not too far away, and here he was, having to rely on second hand radio updates to know what was happening, circling the portal like a caged animal with nowhere to go. Minutes passed by without news, as Mielowa herself waited to hear from the foot soldiers.

An hour went by before, eventually, Faith's voice filled their planes. 'The transporters are landing!' he cried. 'They've cleared the first level!'

'All right,' said Julius, sighing in relief. He knew that the infantry's job had only just started but, as they worked their way down, through the subterranean levels, the ground floor would be able to begin the evacuation. 'Talk to me, Faith.'

'They're loading the Storks and the Herons ... They're starting to take off. Guys, they're on my scanner. The first ships are breaking orbit.'

'Goshawk, this is Commander Fletcher,' said a new voice. 'Arrange your toon along these coordinates, to flank the Storks as they come in.'

'Understood, Sir,' replied Julius. Then he quickly forwarded the location to the others, and took up position near the portal. 'Be ready, everyone.'

As the first Stork approached Sector 7, Julius felt a lump in his throat, as he thought of how close they were to getting some of their people back. He wondered about his parents. Where were they? Was someone taking care of them? He hoped they would be with people they knew from back home. As for Michael's whereabouts ... well, that was everybody's guess.

He watched as the Stork moved closer and closer to the portal; as soon as it entered the green-lit path, it disappeared in a fizz of static discharge before his eyes. 'This is just,' he whispered, in disbelief.

'Unbelievable,' said Morgana, obviously as stunned as he was.

'Look alive, guys,' said Skye. 'There are more incoming.'

Slowly, but steadily, the number of Storks heading for their portal increased, and so did the number of Cougars along the transports routes, which were there to cover them. To actually see them arriving, one after the other, and disappearing like packages at the end of a conveyer belt, made Julius realise that this operation was going to take a long time to complete. He looked at his watch, and noticed that they had been working for almost two hours already. He knew that when his toon needed to re-fuel or rest, they would be recalled to the hangar, while another toon took their place, and so on in rotating shifts as needed, until it was done.

It took the Zed infantry the best part of the next 7 hours to reach the last sub level of the camp. By then, news of a few casualties on both sides had reached Moonrising and the pilots. It understandably dampened the mood and, for a while after, there was virtual silence on the channels, save for vital pieces of information.

At 22:30, Julius and his toon were sitting in their Cougars inside the hangar, ready to begin their third shift after an hour break. He was thinking now about Captain Kelly, wondering where he was, and if he had also infiltrated the site. Julius had seen him in action a couple of times, and he knew that he could fend for himself. Still, he would have hated to hear about anything bad had happening to him. He checked the news screen on his PIP, and scanned the casualty list. As was to be expected, Zed losses were all among the ground troops, and all names that Julius didn't know. But, he knew, they had been students just like him, once upon a time, probably with families to whom they'd never return. Saddened, he selected the mission page, where a counter indicated that 6 million people had been rescued so far. Commander Fletcher had estimated that, all going well, they would finish around midday on Sunday.

Julius' next shift was going to be a shorter one and, at midnight, he would be allowed four hours of sleep. As he sat waiting in his Cougar, before closing his PIP, he went into his messages, opened a new one, on which he wrote one word, "Hey," before sending it to Farrah. 'Toon 4, ready check and stand by,' he said to the others. The lights turned green, and the bridge authorised them for take-off. 'Come on, guys. One more shift till Bedshire.'

Once back out in space, they resumed their positions, replacing one of the toons that was due a break. The Storks were still flowing along to the nearby portal, only with a bit more speed and frequency. Perhaps, after several hours, they had become more efficient at loading passengers, whisking them through to Earth, and making the journey back to here.

'At least Mielowa hasn't reported anyone as missing,' said Morgana.

'Yes,' commented Faith. 'It seems like the portals are working well, thankfully.'

'What about the pilots who are going back and forth?' asked Skye, who was still a little unsure about the new technology.

'Nothing to report on that one either,' answered Faith. 'But we'll probably find out tomor–'

'Faith?' asked Morgana. 'You there?'

'Hmm … that's strange,' he said, after a pause.

'What is?' asked Julius, now fully alert.

'I have a very weird reading coming from the far side of the camp.'

'You do?' asked Isolde. 'And how can you tell from *here*?'

'Faith,' said Julius, 'did you alter the Cougars' long range scanners, by any chance?'

'Maybe ... but that's not the point. I'm telling you, I've picked up something odd, an object of some sort, which has left the camp and is heading east.'

Julius thought about it for a moment, then opened a channel to Commander Fletcher. 'Sir,' he said. 'We're picking up an unusual reading here.'

'What is it, Goshawk?' said Fletcher.

'It looks like an unidentified ship has left the camp, heading east. I'm sending you the trace,' said Julius, transferring Faith's findings.

'You may be right,' said Fletcher. 'Although, how you got this information is beyond me.'

Julius acted innocent, and ignored the last part of his comment.

'I'll go check it out. You guys stay here and keep your eyes open. You're doing a grand job, Toon 4.'

'Aww … That was nice of him,' said Morgana, cheered by the compliment.

'What do you think it was, Faith?' asked Skye.

'Me best guess would be an Arneshian shuttle, trying to sneak away.'

'Why would they do that?' asked Isolde.

'To save their butts?' volunteered Skye. 'It doesn't look like they're winning, does it?'

'Attention pilots,' called Commander Fletcher to all the Cougars in his sector. 'Arneshian shuttle on its way to Sector 7. I'm in pursuit.'

'What?' cried Skye.

Julius frantically began to scan the airspace, but couldn't see anything.

'I've got it!' said Faith. 'Incoming, on these coordinates. Sending them through.'

Julius locked them in to his radar and suddenly a blinking point appeared before him. 'We need to stop the Storks, Faith!'

'I'm on it,' he said. 'Moonrising, this is Baza 4. The Storks must be rerouted: we have an incoming bogey on its way here. Looks like it's heading for the portal.'

'Roger, Baza 4. All Storks are being diverted to adjacent portals. All Mizkis, retreat immediately to Moonrising. All Zed officers, support Commander Fletcher.'

Julius looked at the radar and saw that the Mizkis were following orders on the double, while the officers had gone to Fletcher's aid.

Suddenly, a blinding light flashed past them. Julius had to shield his eyes with his arms, for how strong it was. He blinked and looked at his screen; according to his radar, it had come from the Arneshian shuttle.

'What the heck was that?' shouted Skye.

'A pulse of some kind,' answered Faith. 'And it just knocked down all communication channels. Neither Fletcher, nor Moonrising are responding.'

'Then how come *we're* still talking to each other?' asked Morgana.

'It's 'cause I'm *the* Faith, little lady. Our toon has a special channel,' he added.

Morgana giggled nervously. 'Wait until I tell Siena about this!'

'You do that!' said Faith, enthusiastically.

'Hey,' said Julius, 'who's gonna protect the portal, if we leave too?'

'No one apparently,' replied Isolde. 'Come on, guys. We need to retreat.'

'Julius is right,' said Faith. 'Me radar's reading everyone pursuing the bogey, but no one blocking it, or coming this way. What if they don't catch it before it arrives at the portal?'

'And what do you propose we do?' asked Morgana. 'Park sideways in front of the path?'

'Julius, we need to retreat!' insisted Isolde. 'Clavel was clear, we can't engage the enemy.'

'We're not going to,' he said. 'We'll switch off the portal, instead.'

'What, did you bring a spacesuit or something?' asked Skye.

'He meant with our skills, Dumbo,' said Faith, cheekily.

'I knew that,' answered Skye, vaguely.

'What's the plan, then?' asked Morgana.

'We'll let it get to the portal, and at the last second we cut off the power, so it goes right through it and into the docking bay on the other side. Isolde, will you help us?'

She didn't answer straight away, but eventually replied, 'All right, I'll do it.'

'Good girl,' said Faith, pleased. 'The more, the merrier.'

'Come on then,' said Julius, hurrying them. 'Spread out, around the core of the portal.'

'Which is?' asked Skye.

'It's that large sphere at the centre of the structure, linking the two rings,' answered Faith.

'We need to blow it off,' said Julius, 'but not too early. They must see the green lights, until the very last second.' He positioned his Cougar above the core section, and focused his mind on it, then he took a deep breath and waited. The dot on his radar was drawing closer with every blink. 'Hold it steady,' he said to the others. Out of the corner of his eye, he spotted the Arneshian shuttle approaching fast, pursued by a large number of Cougars. 'Here it comes. Ready … Steady … Now!'

Five yellow beams shot out of the Cougars, striking the portal's core just as the enemy shuttle was about to hit it. There was a small explosion which sent sparks flying, and made the portal shake and wobble. The Arneshian pilot, just as Julius had foreseen, shot straight through and kept on going toward Moonrising. The Zed Cougars had veered off at the last minute, but were now returning to the portal.

Julius watched the enemy shuttle trying to veer upwards, to avoid Moonrising's opened bay, but it was going too fast, and simply didn't have enough time to pull out. A few seconds later, the Arneshian ship was swallowed up by the battlestar. Commander Fletcher, followed by several Cougars, flew straight past Toon 4, and followed into the hangar, probably to make sure that the pilot was apprehended.

'We did it!' cried Morgana.

A Cougar pulled up next to Julius; the pilot, who Julius didn't recognise, gestured for him to go back to Moonrising.

'Guys, we've been recalled,' said Julius. 'Head back to the hangar.' It was then that he noticed something floating upwards from the portal, soon to be lost in space. 'What is that?' he said to himself. He took off after it, trying to get close, but not so close as to touch it with his ship.

'Julius, where are you going?' asked Morgana.

'I'll be right there,' he replied. He was getting ever nearer the object, but couldn't tell exactly what it was, as it spun freely on its own axis, reflecting Moonrising's external lights back at Julius. He locked his mind on it and, using the catalyst, gently pulled it close to him, until it bumped against the Cougar's body, and came to a rest on its nose. He kept it there, using a portion of his powers, making sure to keep enough of his mind focused on piloting the plane back into the hangar. When he climbed out of his cockpit, there was a commotion around the Arneshian plane. He ignored it and called for Faith. 'Can you get that thing down?' he said, pointing at the nose of his Cougar.

'What did you find?' asked Faith, hovering upwards, and reaching for the item. As he landed back on the ground again, Morgana, Skye and Isolde came running towards them.

'It was a holo pilot!' said Morgana. 'As always, they're not brave enough for– Hey! What is that?'

Faith held it out, and they all examined it. The mysterious silver object was cross-shaped, with small cubes, spheres and triangles grouped at the ends of each of its four arms; it was glowing, lit by some sort of internal, green luminescence. In the centre, where the arms met, was a black sphere. The arms had a series of holes along their length, placed at random intervals. Julius noticed how the smaller parts were all assembled symmetrically, following the same pattern: each arm ended in a silver sphere; a triangle grew out of it and, at each of its base corners, was a smaller sphere. From each of these, three further little arms shot out, each terminating in a cube.

'It reminds me of one of those molecular model sets that I used in Chemistry class,' said Faith.

'One section seems to be switched off,' observed Morgana. She pointed at the three cubes at the end of the part in question, and their connecting ball. 'See?'

'I have no idea what it is,' said Julius, after a while. 'But I think it was ejected from the shuttle.'

'Why?' asked Isolde.

'Maybe the pilot didn't want us to find it,' replied Julius.

'Whatever it is, I hope it's good enough to get us out of trouble,' said Skye, looking up. 'Clavel is heading this way, and he doesn't look at all pleased.'

'McCoy! Shanigan!' shouted Clavel striding up to them. 'Cress' office. Now! And bring that thing with you,' he finished, pointing at the mysterious object.

Julius swallowed, and threw a worried glance at Faith.

'Good luck,' whispered Morgana, as they walked away. 'We'll be in the lounge.'

Clavel, who was normally a very peaceful and relaxed man, seemed to have lost all of his usual poise, and was now striding ahead of them, sending red and black wisps every which way.

'*He's really mad*,' said Julius, to Faith, with his mind.

Faith simply nodded, and gulped.

Clavel led them out of Tijara's hangar, and all the way to the front of the ship, where the school staff had their quarters.

Moonrising was still in safe mode so, whatever this place looked like when it was full of colour was anybody's guess. Just now, however, it looked pretty shabby.

They had just taken the corridor which led to Cress's office, when a door swung open and the furious Master jumped out in front of them. 'Inside!' he bellowed.

'Yes, sir,' replied Julius and Faith together, before hurrying after him.

They stood to attention in the middle of the room, while Clavel and Cress towered in front of them.

'The artifact, McCoy!' said Cress.

Julius handed it to him, and watched as the Master placed it delicately on his desk. There was a strange look on his face as he handled it, and a thick green wisp had just emerged from the crown of his head.

'I'm extremely disappointed, and so is Professor Clavel,' said Cress. 'Of all the times you could have chosen to disobey orders and pull one of your stunts, you really picked the wrong one. Explain yourself!'

Julius felt slightly miffed by this particular ticking off. Hadn't they just prevented an enemy ship from entering the portal to Earth? What was he on about? 'Sir, after the pulse attack, we were cut off from Moonrising, and Commander Fletcher. When we saw that the portal was going to be left defenceless we … *I*, gave the order to deactivate it, to prevent the Arneshian's escape. And it worked.'

Cress was breathing deeply through his nostrils now. He made Julius think of a bull who was preparing to charge, which was most unlike the Master of Tijara. Surely there was more to this than he was letting on.

'Let me tell you the story from our perspective, McCoy,' said Cress. 'Toon 4 warns Commander Fletcher of a strange reading, which the officer pursues, as per protocol. And that's OK, because he's trained for it. Then, Toon 4 receives a direct order from the bridge of Moonrising, to pull back, which doesn't happen. And that's not OK, because you lack the training. Orders from superior officers must be followed!'

Julius could see that Cress was getting more worked up with every sentence, and he didn't like where this was going.

'If Mr Shanigan here hadn't tampered with the Cougars' com-links, you would have been able to hear us loud and clear, because, funnily enough, we have the technology to bypass a pulse attack! But *you* couldn't, because *his* system was fighting ours!' he said, pointing at Faith. 'So, Fletcher couldn't tell you to get out of the way, but kept pushing the Arneshian towards the portal, because WE-HAD-A-PLAN! An entire team was waiting for this dratted shuttle on the other side of the portal, ready to catch it, but it never arrived! And, do you know why? Because *you* broke the damn portal! It will take us hours to fix that core engine, delaying the entire mission by half a day! The artifact would have been retrieved on the other side, end of story. Satisfied?'

Julius and Faith just stood there, speechless, trying to digest Cress' words.

'Just who do you think you are?' continued Cress loudly, still in obvious need to let off steam. 'After four years of training, you still treat us like we're the enemy, the people to contradict! There is nothing that we do on Zed that is meant to hurt you. Nothing! We are your family.' And with that, he stomped around the table and sat down in his chair.

'Your flight support to the mission is over,' said Clavel. 'You will assist in the hangar with repairs and maintenance. You will *not* take part in the next rescue mission, whenever that may be and, if needed, the biggest thing you'll fly will be a sky-jet. There will be no leaving Tijara and no access to New Satras until further notice. That goes for the rest of your toon as well.'

'Please, sir!' cried Faith, arms in the air.

'Sir!' started Julius.

'Sir, nothing,' said Clavel. 'They are not puppets. They chose the same way as you did, and so they'll pay the consequences for their actions. You have three hours left before your next shift. I suggest you retire. Dismissed.'

'Yes, sir,' said Julius. He threw a last glance at Cress, and left the room.

'I'm sorry, Julius,' said Faith, as they walked back to the lounge. 'It's all me fault. If I hadn't added that stupid extra channel, we wouldn't be in this mess.'

'If you hadn't added that long range sensor, we would never have caught that shuttle, so don't apologise. Beside, have you seen the way Cress reacted, when he saw that thing?'

'No. What do you mean?'

'Never mind that, now. Cress seemed *thrilled* to have it on his desk. That alone, if you ask me, is the reason why we're not out of the rescue missions altogether, washing Felice's dishes in the galley.'

When they reached the lounge, the rest of the toon was waiting in one of the booths, sipping hot chocolate.

'Go get us a hot drink, and I'll tell them,' said Faith.

Julius nodded, grateful at not having to do that part. When he returned, he realised that Faith hadn't told them either. Not really, anyway. He had recorded the entire scene on his PIP, and was now letting Master Cress do the telling, and the shouting, aided by Clavel.

'Shoot,' said Skye, in frustration. 'Can you believe that? No New Satras? Maintenance duties? No offence, Faith.'

'None taken. And, by the way, Morgana, I wouldn't mention this to Siena.'

'I think the story has already done the rounds twice,' said Morgana. 'Too late, Faith.'

Isolde stood up. 'I should have left when the order came. I feel like it's your fault, Julius, but I have no one to blame but myself.'

'Isolde, I'm sorry,' replied Julius, standing up.

She just looked at him, and left.

'Isolde, wait,' he called.

'Let her go,' said Morgana. 'We're all tired now, and we need some rest. I'll talk to her tomorrow.'

'Here, let me send you a copy of tonight's episode of the Cress' show, in case you can't sleep,' said Faith.

'Gee, thanks,' said Julius. As he opened his PIP to check that it had arrived, he saw a new message from Farrah. He opened it and read, "You. X". He smiled. At least the day was closing on a bit of a high.

CHAPTER 6

NIGHT CRAWLING

Morgana had been right about their story being common knowledge. As soon as they resumed their shift at 4 in the morning, they were welcomed by a few cheers of sympathy from some of their classmates and some not so encouraging looks from the Mizki Seniors. The toon just kept their heads down and took to refueling and repairing the Cougars, avoiding too much banter and generally keeping a low profile.

Julius was particularly annoyed at the New Satras ban, since that was the only place where he could have met up with Farrah. Moreover, Cress' accusations about treating them like they were the enemy still rang in his ears, making him even more upset. Sure enough, in hindsight, he realised he had screwed up royally, but certainly not with the intention of hurting Zed. His intentions had been good; he had just been trying to protect the portal and whoever was on the other side. How could Cress and Clavel not see that? He shook his head, glad at least that Freja hadn't been summoned about this. And — considering it was already the second time that he had been in trouble in the past month — that was a bit of a miracle.

Early Sunday evening, the Oceania Mission officially ended, bringing with it widespread relief and a welcome sense of accomplishment. Moonrising regained its colourful appearance, while a big dinner party was held in Tijara's lounge. Staff and students were finally allowed to relax and exchange their experiences and impressions, while pictures of the Oceanic countries scrolled across the many screens dotted around the ship.

Mielowa was reporting moving stories of people returning to their homes after the many months that had passed. There were tears of joy, and of sadness, as some of them had died in captivity, mainly due to illness or old age. George Lowet and Felicity Steep were both huddled in a booth, talking to their families via their PIPs.

One thing which piqued everyone's curiosity, was that every single one of the rescued Earth folk were wearing Arneshian circlets around their heads, just like the one T'Rogon had been sporting, the previous year. The captive had reported that these circlets shone with some sort of inner light, which went off as soon as they were removed from the compound. None of them were able to offer an explanation for it but, since they were removed with no apparent discomfort to the wearer, the matter was pushed to one side, as nothing more than an Arneshian oddity.

'Last year Michael told me that they wear them to amplify their Grey Skills,' explained Julius.

'But these are humans, with no skills to amplify,' replied Morgana.

'Maybe they wanted everyone to look like them,' offered Skye.

Julius doubted that, but he had no better explanation for it.

That night passed quickly and, at two o'clock, the Mizkis were asked to retire, and were given the Monday off.

'It's so unfair,' Julius said to Skye, once they were back in their room. 'A whole day that I could spend with Farrah, and I'm not even allowed to leave Tijara.'

'Well, at least *one of us* will get to see his lady tomorrow,' said Skye, winking cheekily.

'Still with Valentina, huh?'

'And we'll be celebrating, oh yeah!'

'Great,' huffed Julius. 'Just what I needed to hear.'

'You'd better text Farrah and let her know, by the way.'

'I will,' said Julius. Now that they had made a start of sorts, he certainly didn't want to risk losing her over some silly reason. He opened his PIP and began to type.

The last day of October finally arrived, and Julius headed to Professor Chan's Pyrokinesis class, which was held in a massive area at the back of BM Tijara. Since last year, he had learned to control the amount of fire his body generated and, now that his gene therapy had increased his skill so considerably, Julius was much better at creating the size of fireball he wanted, without singeing Chan's eyebrows.

'Gather up, Mizkis,' called Chan. 'There's something we need to discuss before we start our lesson. Can anyone tell me, is fire able to burn in space?'

Everyone raised their hands.

'Mr Liway?'

'There's no oxygen in space, sir, so if you just have fuel it won't burn.'

'Very good. And why does the Sun, or any of the stars, appear to be *burning* then, Miss Migliori?'

'They don't burn because of a chemical reaction, sir,' explained Siena, 'but by nuclear fusion, where an atom's nucleus bonds with another nucleus; that way, they don't need oxygen. Stars are like nuclear bombs which are continuously exploding, for billions and billions of years.'

'Good,' said Chan. 'Although we tend to stay indoors out here, there may be times where you may need to use this particular skill in open space.'

'We're going nuclear, sir?' asked Faith, worried as usual about them needing any type of augmentation.

'You already *have*, Mr Shanigan. Your Pre-Pyro treatment, last year, has given you the ability to create fusion. Just now, it's lying dormant, and it will remain so, until you need it.'

'He's kidding, right?' Faith whispered sideways to Julius.

'Sir,' said Barth. 'Isn't there a risk that we, you know, end up blowing the whole place up?'

'That would be regrettable, Mr Smit, but the fusion only functions in the vacuum of space, when it detects the absence of oxygen, and it's only as powerful as your own individual Pyro skill.'

'Good,' said Barth, hesitantly. 'It's just that, me being me and all, I'm a little concerned that–'

'I see, Mr Smit, and you may be right,' said Chan, raising an eyebrow. 'I guess it's your choice at this point. Do you want to keep avoiding the challenges that life throws at you, or are you willing to step up to them? Personally, I'd feel safe knowing that you're my navigator, but I'd still like to know that you have at least given this mind-skill a try. Only then will you know if it's for you or not. Remember, we all have talents, and it's our duty to use them. But first, you have to discover those talents.'

Barth stared intently at Chan as he spoke, and Julius noticed a little golden wisp coiling around his classmate's head. 'Good on you, Professor,' he thought to himself. Chan's compliment and words of encouragement had obviously made an impression.

'Now,' resumed Chan, 'after a year of creating fireballs of all different sizes and shapes, I want you to learn how to *direct* these projectiles, using your telekinetic skills. Split up into your usual range groups and pick a lane.'

Julius joined the 300 + feet group, which was made up of Leanne Nord, Felicity Steep, Ferenc Orban, Kaleb Kashny, and Isolde. He let them go first, they all managed to generate their fireballs, and releasing them, but they weren't able to guide them at all.

After several unsuccessful attempts, Ferenc turned to Julius. 'What am I doing wrong?'

Julius was surprised that *he* was the one being asked like that, what with Professor Chan just at a few feet away from them. He stood, and walked up to the line, vaguely aware that Isolde was still giving him the cold shoulder, annoyed as she was about their ongoing detention. 'I think you need to release it slowly, so you can actually guide it. If you're too fast, it's harder to control.'

'Show me,' said Ferenc.

The others made space, leaving Julius alone at the front of the lane. He took up his usual stance: right hand lifted, palm facing up and bent slightly outwards. He could feel the energy starting to flow through his veins, converging towards the palm of his hand. He had learned to be careful about how much of this energy he let out because, having to reduce the size of the fireball after release, which required drawing some of the power back in, caused a painful burning sensation all up his arm.

Once he had created a sphere the size of a football, he pulled his hand back, then forward, and gently released it; the ball floated forward steadily away from him. He locked his mind on it, and guided it first up, then downwards and finally to the left and right. When it reached the end of the lane he summoned it back to him, this time making it follow an undulating line. To finish off, he pushed it up above his head and slapped it forward like a volleyball. The fireball disintegrated an instant later against the far wall.

Happy with the performance, he turned around, and realised that the entire class was watching, with gaping mouths.

'McCoy, you've just invented a new game,' said Faith, excitedly. 'Professor! We should have a school competition, a tournament of fire-volleyball. And the final can be in space, like a nuclear final!'

Chan stared at Faith, with an intense monobrow.

'Or not ...' added Faith. 'I'll shut up, now,' he finished, and resumed his training.

Julius' group was extremely eager to learn how he had done that, all except for Isolde, who had moved off to train by herself, without a word to anyone else.

'What's her problem?' wondered Julius, shrugging his shoulders. Whatever it was, he decided it was just going to have to take care of itself. After all, he already had Farrah to think about, and Morgana to look after, so he really didn't need to worry about Isolde too.

When the first weekend of December arrived, Julius tried to distract himself by going to the gym and working out until he was completely exhausted. He would have invited the others, but they were nowhere to be found.

It was only on Saturday afternoon that Faith joined him at the dojo, just as Julius was emerging from the changing room. 'There you are!' said Faith. 'I've been looking everywhere for you.'

'Just passing time, really,' said Julius, grabbing his bag. 'The others?'

'Skye's been practicing mouth-to-mouth with Valentina all day, and will probably continue to do so for the rest of the weekend. I was fixing Cougars, *supervised*,' he added, with a grunt.

'Morgana with Isolde?'

'Isolde was with Siena, actually. I haven't seen Morgana since last night.'

That was strange, thought Julius. Maybe she was having some time off, meditating in a holosuite or something.

They headed to the lounge and, while Faith went to fetch them a couple of cold drinks, Julius plunged himself onto one of the sofas, feeling particularly tired and achy. Had Cress *really* said that the ban from Satras applied through December too? Maybe they had misheard him; as desperate as it was, Julius thought he'd check the recording again, just to be sure. He opened his PIP and played the video back. As the camera's point of view was from Faith's palm — who had understandably been trying to be inconspicuous about it — the angle was a little odd, and at times fixed on Master Cress' crotch, which Julius really didn't have any interest in staring at. So he let his eyes wander around the room, checking the shelves, the decor and the pictures on the wall. Finally, it arrived at the bit he was looking for, and Clavel clearly said: "No access to New Satras until further notice. That goes for the rest of your toon as well."

Right then, in the video, Faith threw his arms in the air; as he did this, Julius was given a brief glimpse of Cress' desktop from above, which had several electronic folders moving across the display that was its top. 'Freeze,' he cried, suddenly. He magnified the still a little and had a closer look. There was no mistaking it: one of the files clearly had "Mc-Coy – Classified" written across its cover.

'What's with that face?' said Faith, as he arrived. He placed the glasses down on the table next to the sofa and leaned over to have a look at Julius' PIP.

'I have no idea *what* it is,' replied Julius, pointing at the folder. 'Can you make it clearer?'

Faith sat down on the edge of the sofa, called up the video, and got Julius to show him the point that had caught his attention. He tried out a few of his software add-ons on the footage, and was able to make the image slightly larger. 'This is the best I can do,' he said finally, showing it to Julius.

There was no doubting what the file title read, but why was it there and, more importantly, why was it classified? 'I want to find that file and read it. Tonight, at dinner time,' said Julius, firmly.

'Excuse me! You want to break into Cress' office? Am I hearing you right?'

'The info in there is about me. I want to know what it's about. And anyway, can't we access his terminal from here?'

'We? I'm getting the feeling that you want this detention to last *forever*.' He stared at his friend for a moment, who was unflinching in his resolve. He sighed in resignation. 'All right, I'll help you access his desk, but we need to be *inside* his office. On Satras we could have used any public terminal, but from here they'll trace us in a sec.'

Julius nodded. Faith was right — this wasn't going to be easy.

'Don't these people ever sleep?' said Faith, hovering along in front of Julius, that night.

It was 20:00 hours, and most of the staff were at dinner. Now that Moonrising was out of safe mode, the colours had returned, allowing them to see just how beautifully decorated the staff and officers' quarters really were. They had reached the front portion of Tijara, walking along casually enough, but making sure to be quiet about it. It had been agreed that they would pretend to actually have business with one of their teachers, if anybody decided to stop them.

'The office is along the next corridor to the right,' said Julius.

'Shoot,' said Faith, through gritted teeth. 'Officer coming this way.'

Julius had a quick look, and continued walking casually forward. 'Cress is going to be very pleased when he sees this report, won't he?' he said, loudly.

Faith cottoned on straight away, and maintained the act. 'Of course he will. Besides, he did ask us to *personally* deliver it to him when it was ready.'

'Yes,' said Julius, smiling in the direction of the officer as they passed him. 'He wanted us, *personally*.'

'Evening, sir,' said Faith, bowing his head.

The officer bowed back, but didn't give them a second look.

'That was lucky,' said Julius. 'Come on, we're here.' They turned into the corridor and walked up to the door of the office.

'Knock,' said Faith, 'just like we rehearsed.'

Julius rapped on the door, but there was no answer from inside.

'Let's hope he's eating a big meal,' said Faith. He quickly set to hack the entry mechanism, and a few seconds later they had access.

Julius waited for his friend to go inside, then closed the door behind him, and began to wait. He took a seat on one of the chairs along the corridor, which was sheltered by a large, holographic pot plant. If someone should happen to pass by, he wouldn't be noticed. As the minutes ticked away, he kept nervously checking the time; he hoped Faith would be able to find the file without too many difficulties. 'Come on, Faith,' he whispered.

A few moments later, his PIP bleeped to signal an incoming message. He opened it quickly and grinned. It was a copy of the file. He leapt up and moved to the end of the corridor, to check that the coast was clear, but as he put his head around the corner he practically smacked straight into Cress' chest.

'McCoy,' said Cress, in surprise. 'What are you doing here?'

'I'm sorry, sir,' said Julius, bowing. 'I was looking for you.'

'Right, let's go to my office then,' said Cress, striding to the door.

'Oh, it won't take long, sir,' said Julius, loudly, hoping that Faith would hear him and find a place to hide.

'What is it?'

'I would like to ask you to lift the ban from New Satras ...' began Julius, but when he saw Cress' face growing thunderous, he changed tactic, '... for my toon, sir. It wasn't their idea. I was their leader and they obeyed orders. They've paid enough for it, sir.'

Cress looked at him, dubiously. 'Very well. But the ban is still in place for you and Mr Shanigan, until I see fit to lift it.' And with that he turned and entered his office.

Julius ran to the door, waiting to hear shouting or cries coming from inside, but there was total silence. He tried to focus on Faith and searched for his friend's mind, calling out to him mentally. *'Faith ... Can you hear me?'*

A faint answer carried to him, and he honed in on it. *'Faith?'*

'I can hear you. Did you get the file?'

'Yes. Where are you?'

'I'm lying on the floor, between the sofa and the wall,' he replied angrily. *'Can't you get him out of this room?'*

'What is he doing?'

'How should I know? All I can see is the blinking ceiling!'

'OK, OK. I'll think of something, but it may take a while.'

'Whatever you do, do it fast. And don't even think about leaving me here all night!'

'The guy is gonna need to sleep at some point,' said Julius, defensively. 'Oh no!'

'What? What's happening?'

'Foster is staring right at me …'

'Julius, no! Don't you dare …'

'Good evening, Captain Foster,' said Julius, 'I was just with Master Cress and heading back to my quarters.'

Foster looked at him, with the special suspicious look he reserved only for members of the Skirts. 'Move along,' he growled.

Julius bowed and left, aware that the captain was only a few steps behind him. 'Poor Faith,' he thought. There was nothing else to do, so he went up to the lounge, hoping that Cress would go to bed soon.

With no Morgana or Skye in sight, he grabbed an empty booth and opened up his PIP to read the file, being careful to shield it from any nearby Mizkis. The cover was exactly like he'd seen in Faith's video before, with a tiny little symbol at the bottom, 4 stars connected by lines to form a diamond; he opened the folder with a flick of his finger. There was only one document in it, and it was all about him. Across the page, a red APPROVED seal stood out clearly. Both Freja and Cress had signed it. Julius focused on the main text. In it, the Grand Master was discussing the fact that, after four years of observation and intense gene therapy, Julius was the ideal and only candidate for Tijara's Heart. Confused, Julius continued reading. They obviously wanted him to take part in some sort of mission, but then, why hadn't they told him about it? Cress had talked a lot about how important communication between the head staff and the Mizkis was, yet now it seemed that Cress was the first to hold back. Annoyed, Julius scanned the rest of the paragraph, but found nothing worth remembering. As he reached the end of the document his eyes stopped on an added comment at the bottom of the page, which he definitely wasn't expecting to find there. It read, "Keep him away from FH as much as possible". Only one person, among Julius' friends at least, had those initials, and that was Farrah: Farrah Hendricks. Completely baffled, he re-read the document, making sure there was nothing else attached.

It was almost midnight when Faith showed up at Julius' booth, carrying a tray of whatever food he'd been able to find at that hour.

'Sorry, mate,' said Julius. 'Foster did his best.'

'I know,' answered Faith. 'But you owe me one, big time.'

'For sure. How did you get out?'

'You don't want to know. Anyway, was it worth it?'

Julius thought about it, then sent him the file. 'See for yourself.'

Discreetly, Faith opened his own screen and began to read. 'What's this symbol, on the cover?'

'Don't know. And before you ask, I also don't know what they're talking about.'

Faith scoured the file; when he saw the last line he looked up. 'Can this be your girlfriend they're talking about?'

'She's not my *girlfriend*, actually. But she is the only one I know with those initials.'

'But why? Surely you can date whoever you want?'

'Who said anything about *dating*?'

Faith looked at him blankly.

'OK, maybe,' admitted Julius. 'But it beats me why it can't be her. Anyway, I guess you heard Cress' answer about the ban.'

'Yep. Skye and Morgana will be happy.'

'Isolde too. She's been a right grouch lately.'

'It's because she likes you,' said Faith, simply. 'She wants to hate you for the mess you got her into, but she also wants to suck your lips off. And that makes her all sour-faced.'

'You've been spending too much time with Miller, you know?'

'Skye? Not likely. If I ever need advice, I'd feel safer asking Morgana, I think. She's got that female insight thingy and she's getting loads of practice lately, if you get me drift,' he said, chuckling. He quickly stopped though, when he saw how unamused Julius' was. 'Uh, heh. Just kidding …'

Skye, Morgana and Isolde had, of course, been grateful to Julius and Faith, for the lift on their bans. Julius knew that Morgana would once again start disappearing off to meet Maks whenever she could, which made him wonder what exactly had possessed him to request some leniency from Cress as he had, and not something else entirely.

Naturally, they were also curious to hear all about Julius' classified file, and tried their best to figure out what it could possibly mean, but without success. When Julius shared the note at the bottom of the page, Morgana didn't say anything, while Skye made similar comments to the ones made by Faith.

Fortunately, Julius was soon distracted from thoughts of bans and detentions, as Moonrising was treated to the news that the next planet had been located for the second of their rescue missions. Although there was no information as to how Zed had found it, the little luscious planet stood at the center of a small solar system, in the Capricornus constellation. Thrilled by their success with Oceania, Mizkis and officers alike were rearing to take it on. As

November got underway, more details about the mission began to emerge, until finally it was confirmed that there were about 600 million bio-signatures on the planet.

'Professor Clavel, do we know who they are?' asked Faith, during a piloting lesson.

Clavel was still upset with the Skirts, but he was their teacher after all, and therefore treated them the same as always. 'If the Arneshians are indeed keeping them grouped by continent, we can guess from the number that they may be from the Americas. But we haven't established that yet.'

'I hope so,' said Lopaka. 'My folks would be there at least — that is, if they've put the Hawaiians in with the rest of them.'

'Mine will be there,' said Leanne, without her usual brio. 'My whole family lives in Canada.'

'What about you Mizkis?' Clavel asked, looking at Manuel Valdez and Evita Suarez.

'Yes,' answered Evita, 'mine are all in Argentina.'

'Mexico and Peru,' said Manuel. 'They should be there.'

'This one is going to last for ages,' commented Skye.

'About a month, Mr Miller. Imagine if we had to do it centuries ago, when the population was *twice* that number.'

'At least now we know what to expect,' said Lopaka.

'I wouldn't be too sure, Mr Liway,' said Clavel. 'This mission is far bigger and this time the Arneshians will be expecting us. Security will be tighter, mark my words.'

'What's our plan, sir?' asked Morgana.

'We need to stay out of scanner range for the moment. Scouts will be deployed to assess the situation from within. We need to know what our infantry will be facing when they land. Planning is ever more important this time around, Miss Ruthier.'

The seriousness in Clavel's voice had dampened their spirits somewhat, so the students returned to studying flight tactics scenarios, harder than ever.

'I wonder who they'll send to infiltrate the settlement,' said Julius.

'Whoever they are, it's a dangerous job,' said Morgana.

'But also exciting,' added Skye.

'I hate waiting,' said Julius, frustrated. 'We don't even know if they'll let us take part at all. And if they do, we're either gonna be in here, fixing engines, or out there on a sky-jet!'

'It's done, now,' said Morgana. 'Let it go, Julius.'

Julius was really looking forward to seeing the back of this year, which had been one of the toughest he had ever experienced.

News relating to the rescue mission had become increasingly rare, to the point where even Mielowa had started to urge the Curia to release any information they had on the scouting plan, to appease Moonrising's unsettled crew.

Julius spent most of his free time practicing sky-jet manoeuvres with the Skirts, or in the gym working out. Every day he would also text Farrah, although he tried not to overdo it, under Skye's advice. That was easier said than done though, especially every time Morgana announced that she was off to dinner with Maks, or going to take a walk with Maks, or going shopping with Maks. Julius had to admit it, at least to himself: it wasn't easy letting someone else look after her, no matter how hard he tried.

The evening of Sunday, the 30th of December, was one such night. They had tried coming up with new ways of using sky-jets in combat since earlier in the day, and by 20:00 they were getting tired and quite stroppy.

'That's enough for today, guys,' said Morgana, picking up her bag. 'I need to go get changed.'

'But we haven't finished yet,' said Julius. 'We've still got the last scenario to run through.'

'I'm tired,' said Morgana, 'I can't focus anymore and I'm late.'

'Late for what?' asked Julius, sounding more annoyed than was necessary.

'Late for a *date*, if you must know.'

'You're spending enough time with Maks as it is these days, doing Zed knows what, while we need to practice these formations.'

'I resent what you're implying,' cried Morgana.

'I wasn't implying, I was telling!'

'I know what I'm doing, thank you very much!' replied Morgana, outraged. 'And one more thing, mind your own business!' With that, she stormed out of the hangar, without looking back.

'Ouch…' said Skye. You really have a way with women, McCoy.'

'I felt the chill right down me bones, so I did,' added Faith, with a shiver.

'You shouldn't talk,' snapped Julius. 'What have *you* done about Siena, huh? Nothing, that's what.'

'I'm getting there,' said Faith, defensively.

'Cut it out, you two,' said Skye. 'Let's just go to eat before I lock you both inside the sim-dating programme.'

Julius agreed that the sensible thing to do right now, so he switched off the desktop screen and picked up his bag.

'McCoy,' called Mr Simmons, a short, bald engineer, who was in charge of the sky-jet sector. He walked briskly towards them. 'Before you go, the Ahura Mazda needs a few sky-jets onboard. Can you guys deliver them?'

Julius looked at the others, grinning. 'Of course we can, sir.'

'Very well. The ship is just outside our docking bay. Don't keep her waiting.'

'We're on it!' whooped Faith.

The three of them ran toward their sky-jets, their hunger and tiredness forgotten.

'We may even get to see Captain Kelly,' said Julius.

'I hope so,' answered Skye, hopping onto one of the jets. 'Imagine if he invites us to stay for New Year!'

'That would be awesome!' agreed Julius. 'Goshawk, ready to go,' he said, lifting off.

'Baza, ready,' said Faith.

'Vulture, ready,' said Skye.

'Let's go,' called Julius, excited to be finally doing something useful.

They passed through the protective membrane and were soon out in space. The Ahura Mazda was literally in front of them and, although Julius was itching to take his jet for a ride, he knew that he had to make the delivery without any delays, so he headed for the ship's docking bay.

Once all three of them had entered, the port below them closed, and the bay was re-pressurised. When the light turned green, Julius knew it was safe to remove the jet's protective cupola.

'Welcome aboard,' Captain Kelly greeted them, and bowed.

Julius, Faith and Skye bowed back, before breaking into large smiles.

'It's good to see you again, boys,' said Kelly, amiably.

'Good to see you too, Captain,' said Julius. He had always liked Kelly. In a strange sense that he couldn't explain, the captain felt like a big brother to Julius, and even more strangely, he felt the sudden urge to tell him *everything* about Farrah.

'Come eat with us,' he said. 'Elian would love to see you.'

The boys looked at each other, obviously eager to stay.

'Could someone tell Mr Simmons, in engineering, please?' asked Julius. 'We … um … are already in a spot of trouble with Cress and … um … could do without the aggravation?'

Kelly let out one of his booming laughs, and patted Julius hard on the shoulder. 'I'll take care of it, but I want to hear all about it. Come on up.'

Julius and the others followed him up to the mess hall, unable to believe their luck at being on the Ahura Mazda again. 'I bet Morgana will be *furious* when she finds out,' thought Julius, feeling a little pleased about that.

Elian was indeed happy to see them, and the whole crew made them feel right at home. Julius was, of course, no stranger to them, and Skye and Faith had been on board long enough to remember their way around.

Kelly chatted away to them, asking all about how things were going on Moonrising. As soon as he heard that they didn't have any plans for New Year, he called the battlestar's engineer, requesting the boys' presence on board for active duties, as well as training, for the whole weekend.

Mr Simmons saw no reason to refuse the captain's request, and wrote a note next to their names, in the Tijaran manifest, so that if someone came looking for them, they would know where they were.

With that out of the way, the evening got properly started. Skye was entertaining half of the male crew, with stories of his various conquests, and all about the creation of the sim-dating programme, which had been built under his specifications — a piece of news that immensely raised his status among the Ahura's officers. Faith was deep in conversation with the engineers, telling them about his entry into Pit-Stop Pete's competition, of which he hadn't heard much lately, but that he was sure would grant him at least second place nonetheless.

Julius, Kelly and Elian moved to the bridge after dinner, where there was a beautiful view of the planet where the humans were being held. The indoor lights were switched off, so they could properly admire the star-ridden space outside.

Eventually, later on in the evening, Elian stretched in her chair, then sat up. 'How is Morgana?' she asked. 'I was surprised not to see her with you tonight.'

'She, uh, had to go away, so when they told us to make the delivery she wasn't around,' he said, unwilling to add anything else.

'I see,' she said, standing up. 'You tell her I was asking after her.'

'I will.'

'Goodnight Julius, I'll see you tomorrow.'

'Goodnight, Lieutenant.'

'I'll be right back,' said Kelly, following her out of the room, his aura wrapped in pink wisps.

Curious, Julius peeked over the back of his chair, as inconspicuously as he could, and peered down the dim corridor beyond the exit. It was quite dark, but the vibrancy of the colourful wisps laced among the shadows left no room for doubt; as his eyes adjusted to the dark, he could just about make out Kelly holding Elian, tight in his arms, and kissing her with such passion that Julius was startled for a moment. He quickly turned in his chair to face the front again, feeling his cheeks flushing.

Kelly returned, minutes later, and took his seat again. 'So, how have things been, apart from the detention?'

'Good,' said Julius, trying not betray his surprise at what he had just witnessed. 'I'm still Dr Walliser's lab-rat, but at least now they've got their dosage right, so I don't *interfere* with the running of the ship. Lessons are good too. I like Pyrokinesis and I wish we could do more Twist lessons, but we hadn't had a chance lately, with all this going on.'

'Yeah, I liked that subject too. And how's mad Chan?'

'Still mad,' said Julius, grinning. 'I bet that man would survive anything.'

'We should send *him* to scout the planet, I'm telling you.'

'Yes, we should.'

'You look bulkier, McCoy. Have you been working out?'

'You think so?' asked Julius, flexing his bicep. 'I don't know what else to do. Between Chan's hardcore lessons and the ban from New Satras, I've got plenty of spare time.'

'It doesn't hurt taking care of your body but, what do you mean, nothing else to do? You not seeing anyone?'

'Well, sort of,' he replied. 'There's this girl, from Sield, and she's … she's …' At that point, totally unable to describe her any further without embarrassing himself, he decided to just show Kelly the only picture he had of her. 'Here,' he said, holding the PIP screen up to Kelly. 'This is Farrah Hendricks.'

Kelly looked at the picture, and let out a long whistle. 'Wow, and what exactly have you done to deserve *her*?'

'I know, right?' said Julius, pleased that Kelly approved. 'And I forgot to mention, she's the new Solo champion.'

'So, are you guys going out?'

'We've only met once … and a half. Plus texts.'

'What?'

'Long story, but I was trying to ask her out, when the alarm went off and the mission started. Then I got the detention. But she wants to see me again, and she let me hold her hand, and she said she'll come out to eat with us!'

'It looks like someone is in love, to me,' said Kelly, cheekily.

Julius was surprised to realise that he didn't mind the captain saying that, even though he couldn't quite put a word to his feelings just yet. 'I don't know if it's *love*, but I sure like her … a lot.'

'I bet you do. The room is dark and I can see you glowing red like a little campfire.'

'Although, I don't know why, but I feel that … some people wouldn't like that.'

'It wouldn't be the first time, trust me.'

'Hmm?'

'Never mind,' said Kelly. 'If you like her, just go for it. Some things are worth fighting for. That's a lesson I learned the hard way.' Kelly stood up and walked to the window. 'We'll use the sky-jets to approach the planet. We need something small and undetectable to reach the security tower. Once there, we can teleport a com-link inside the camp, and find out what's going on. We have a few hard weeks ahead of us.' He turned to Julius. 'You can have your old room if you like, unless you want to bunk with your mates.'

'I'll stay with them, thanks. It was good to see you again, Captain.'

'Goodnight, kiddo.'

Julius went back to the room he had shared with Skye and Faith, two years ago, thinking about how things had changed since then. His friends were already fast asleep. As he lay down for the night, his mind wandered to Kelly and Elian, embracing in the shadows of the corridor, only it wasn't really *them* he saw, but himself and Farrah. 'A man's gotta dream,' he thought. With those pleasant images in his head, he drifted off to sleep.

CHAPTER 7

THINGS WORTH FIGHTING FOR

'I will not let you risk your life like that, Elian!'

Julius sat up in bed, startled out of sleep by the shouting, and in his disorientated state, tried to place the source of the voice. It seemed to have come from the corridor. There was no mistaking that it had been Captain Kelly.

'Wha–' started Faith.

'Shhh!' said Julius.

'You have no right to keep me behind!' shouted Elian.

Skye had now also woken up, and was avidly listening to the exchange.

'I believe I do, actually. We have no idea what's waiting for us in that tower, and I don't intend for *you* to find out. End of story,' said Kelly.

'I am an officer too, JD, and I will not step down just because we ... we ... you know.'

Skye looked at Julius, puzzled, who indicated that Elian and Kelly were together, by nodding and tapping the sides of his index fingers together a few times.

'It's my job to protect you, Elian. Call me selfish, but I won't put your life at risk. And that's an order!'

'Any of these guys' lives are just as important as mine!'

'That's not the point!'

'You're their captain!'

'And you're my wife!'

'No way,' gasped Faith.

Julius realised that he was munching away at his fingernails, completely caught up in the argument.

Silence followed Kelly's last statement, save for a few thumps and bumps.

'What's happening?' whispered Skye, eager to hear more. 'Where are they? What are they doing?' He moved to the door and pressed his ear to it.

Julius and Faith followed suit, scampering over each other to get a better ear position. It was at that point that one of them accidentally bumped the door release button, which caused it to zip open sideways, sending all three of them tumbling out into the corridor, where they landed in a heap.

When Julius looked up, Kelly and Elian were staring at them, wrapped in each other's arms.

'Top of the morning, Captain,' said Faith, cheerily, from the bottom of the pile. 'Lieutenant! You look radiant as ever. May I add our sincere congrats for such a happy event?'

Julius scampered to his feet, and gave Skye and Faith a hand up. 'Sorry, we kinda heard ... from the room.'

Elian smiled. 'It's our fault, really. Besides, I'm glad someone finally knows.' She threw a sideways glance at Kelly and walked away.

'We forgot you guys were here. This wing has been empty for a while,' explained Kelly. 'I would appreciate ... er ... if you would keep this to yourselves, please.'

'You don't need to worry about us, Captain,' said Skye. 'Kudos to you! She's your perfect match.'

'Try telling that to my dad,' replied Kelly.

'Is *that* why she said we're the only ones who know?' asked Julius.

Kelly nodded, looking a little downcast.

'No wonder she's pi- ahem, upset,' said Skye, matter-of-factly. 'Women love to spread the news about things like this. Come, Captain,' said Skye, leading Kelly along the corridor. 'Let's go get a coffee, shall we? There's a couple of things you need to know.'

'How old are you, kid?' said Kelly, still being pushed gently forward by Skye.

'Old enough,' he replied, reaching up and patting Kelly's shoulder. 'Old enough.'

Julius stood speechless in the middle of the corridor, watching as the two of them disappeared from sight.

Faith moved over to his side. 'I wonder how long it'll take Miller to realise he's only wearing his underpants.'

After breakfast, Kelly had plenty to attend to on the war deck, so he asked the Skirts to show his ground troops the latest upgrades for the new sky-jets. The crew was to be divided into small groups, with each of them receiving a 30-minute lesson at some point that morning.

When the first team arrived, Julius and Skye stepped back, allowing Faith to lead the session. As he hovered beside one of the scooters, surrounded by ten officers, he demonstrated everything that was new to these models, and fielded all questions professionally and with ease.

'The sky-jets you've been using so far,' explained Faith, 'required you to wear a spacesuit. With these models, you don't have to, because they have the cupola, which keeps you protected against outer space.'

'He really knows his stuff, doesn't he?' whispered Skye to Julius.

'He's a Skirt, after all,' answered Julius.

'Now, if my esteemed colleagues would like to step up to their jets,' said Faith, 'you can split into three groups and practice departure procedures.'

Julius and Skye were more than happy to oblige, as they were finally beginning to feel useful for something actually related to the next mission.

The morning passed quickly, and they were eager to continue straight after lunch.

At 17:00, the last group came in, accompanied by Elian.

'I know I'm not allowed to go,' she said quietly to the Mizkis, 'but I can at least have the training, right?'

Faith started the lesson for the last time that day, and was grateful for it too, as he was starting to feel pretty tired.

'This here is the com-link that one of you will be taking to the tower,' he said to the group. 'It has been adjusted so that it can self-teleport from the tower into the main compound. Captain Kelly needs you to activate the terminal inside the tower, use the map it contains to find a safe internal location, then input those co-ordinates into this com-link, and send it to said location, where hopefully it will be used by our people to contact Moonrising.'

'Thanks for the briefing, Chief,' said Elian, with a smile.

'Very welcome,' replied Faith, grinning.

'How many people can you seat on one of these jets?' asked a black-haired officer.

'Ideally, just one, although, if necessary, you can have two,' answered Faith. 'But it's not very comfy. Look,' he said, sitting down on the jet, with his skirt retracted. 'McCoy, come here.'

Julius hurried over and sat behind him, keeping his feet inside as much as possible, so that Faith could activate the cupola.

As the glass closed over them, there was a snapping sound, and the two boys found themselves with very little space to move in.

'You look like the inside of a can of tuna,' said Skye, chuckling.

'Yeah,' said Julius, with his head squashed against the glass. 'Not comfy, is about right. Can you let us out now?'

'Agreed,' said Faith, whose nose was pressed against the front screen. 'Just a sec 'cause it's not working.'

'Are you OK, guys?' asked Elian, walking over to them.

Skye and the officers were practically howling with laughter by this point, although one of them did manage to control himself enough to lend a hand.

'I think me skirt is stuck in something,' said Faith.

'All right, don't panic,' said Elian, trying to maintain a straight face. 'I'll go get some tools and be right back.'

Skye, in the meantime, decided this was the perfect opportunity for the officers to take a few pictures of him, sitting atop the cupola, above the tangled bodies of his mates. 'I'll make a few bucks from these, thank you very much.'

'Wait until I get out!' cried Julius, shaking his fist in the air, all of about 0.10 inch away from his head, which was as much space as was left in the cupola-cage.

'Relax, McCoy,' said Skye, stretching out over the cupola, with a teasing smile. 'We'll use the money to go out for dinner, with our ladies, you know?'

Faith was banging his head against the glass, in protest, which was pretty much all he could do.

Just as Elian returned to the docking bay, the lights went out, and were replaced by dim, backup ones. Everyone stopped laughing at once.

'What's happening?' asked Skye.

Elian touched the com-link on her chest. 'Bridge, report.' There was no answer, so she ordered the officers to go and check it out. 'Skye, go with them, and send me the Chief. We need to get your friends out of that sky-jet, double-quick.'

Skye nodded, threw one last glance at his mates, and joined the officers.

'Bridge, come in,' continued Elian, growing frustrated. Again, there was no reply, so she plucked up an Omni-gizmo and set to work at the front panel of the jet. 'I'm going to bypass the safety mech–'

Just then, there was an almighty rumble, which shook the whole ship. Elian fell to the floor, still holding onto the tool.

'Elian!' cried Julius.

A siren began to blare, signalling that the ship had entered into a state of red alert.

Elian sat up, and massaged her left arm. She turned her head towards the entrance, and a look of panic washed over her face. Julius followed her gaze and instantly understood: a red light was flashing above the closed door, which meant that the room had automatically sealed itself off from the rest of the ship, and was losing pressure. He would have no time to use his mind-skills. 'Get on the sky-jet!' he shouted desperately to her.

Elian leapt up, sprinted to the nearest scooter, hopped on and activated the cupola, not a moment too late, as the trapdoor below them began to open. The ensuing vacuum sucked the jets up and spun them out into space.

It took a couple of frantic minutes before Faith was able to regain control and, when he did, he quickly realised that they were now far away from the Ahura Mazda, and that the ship was under attack.

'Fly close to Elian, Faith!' urged Julius. Then he sent a mind-message to her. '*What is your tag-name?*'

'*Aurora!*' came the reply.

Julius repeated the name to Faith, who typed it onto the control screen, before opening up a channel.

Faith zoomed over to her; when she spotted him, she came about, beside his jet.

'Elian, are you OK?' asked Julius through their newly opened channel.

'Yes, I am,' she said. 'But we can't stay here, or we'll get caught in the crossfire. We've ended up in the Arneshians airspace, and they could be on us at any moment.'

'Where do we go?' asked Julius.

'Faith? Do you still have the com-link for the mission?'

'Yeah, it's in here.'

'Then let's not waste this opportunity and start the scouting mission, pronto.'

The determination in her voice was enough for Julius. 'Let's do it.'

'Faith, turn off your lights and follow my tracks precisely,' she said. 'Julius, keep your eyes open.'

'Roger, Aurora,' responded Faith, pressing several buttons on his screen.

'Roger that; will do … if I can turn my head, that is,' said Julius. He could just about see the dark bulk of Moonrising, getting smaller as they moved further away from it. The Ahura Mazda, and the attacking Arneshian ships, were now directly behind them so he had lost sight of them completely. 'Faith, can we contact the captain?'

'Elian's sent him a distress call already. Let's hope he picks it up soon, even though he *has* more pressing matters at hand.'

Julius tried to pull his head up as much as possible, so he could turn it both ways. A wave of Cougars was flying in their direction, engaging any enemy ships that were trying to come at them. Below him, the planet was getting closer. Even without the aid of scanners, he could tell there was a large deployment of Arneshian ships, and they were waiting for the assault to start.

'I can see the camp from here,' said Faith. 'It's massive.'

'It's a big mission,' answered Elian. 'I've sent you the coordinates of our landing point. Can you see it?'

'Yes, it's flashing.'

'Good, stay with me.' Elian took them by the most hidden way she could find, skirting past debris, and in and out of tunnels of meteorites. She used every natural shelter she could find, to protect them from any stray hits, and from being spotted.

Julius could see now that she was a natural pilot, just like Morgana and, given their predicament, he was grateful that Faith was able to keep up with her so well. After a while of this, the tower came into view; they drew closer and continued past it for about 2,000 yards, before slowly lowering their altitude. Julius could see that there was some sort of energy field covering the holding area like a dome and assumed that it worked in much the same way as the Zed shield did. After all, if humans were being kept there, they would need oxygen to breathe.

The scooters landed in among thick bushes, which consisted of exotic plants, the likes of which Julius had never seen before.

The leaves were blue-grey, rather than the green that they were all accustomed to, creating an eerie atmosphere. Tall trunks grew at odd angles, forming an impressive barrier, almost impossible to penetrate. Using the cascading foliage as cover, Elian inched her sky-jet slowly forward, closely followed by the boys, until they were in sight of the rectangular tower beneath the protective shield. 'This is it,' she said. 'According to our initial readings, the structure itself is empty, save for the backup terminals.'

'How do we know that we won't set off any alarms, by going in?' asked Julius, over the com-channel.

'We don't. I'll go first and, if all's well, you follow. If not, drive the other way, as fast as you can.'

'No way!' said Faith. 'Kelly would kill us if he found out we'd abandoned you like that!'

'Well, he won't. And, it's an order,' she replied.

Julius focused ahead, into the distance, and saw that there were several guards patrolling the compound. He sighed. He hated it when adults pulled rank like Elian had just done. Why was it that only grown-ups got to do all the dangerous stuff?

Elian began to move forward again, towards a spot far away from the guards. As the nose of her jet touched against the shield, there was no resistance, so she pressed on. To their relief, no alarm sounded. 'You can enter now,' she said.

Faith pushed toward the same portion of shield and they were soon through it without being detected.

They came to a stop, and the boys watched as Elian climbed off her jet. She had the Omni-gizmo tool in her hand and, as she reached them, she knelt in front of their scooter and started to tamper with the safety mechanism. A few minutes later, there was a click, and the cupola vanished. Faith almost fell out onto the ground, but Julius caught him at the last minute. He let go of his friend, once he had steadied him, and they eased out of the vehicle. Julius stood and stretched out his arms and legs, to get the blood circulating again.

'You guys up for some telekinesis?' asked Elian. 'We need to hide these two jets in the bushes somewhere.'

Both Julius and Faith nodded eagerly and, starting with their own jet, they locked their minds on it and shifted it back outside the shield, where they manoeuvred it out of sight, behind a large purple bush.

Once the second jet had been hidden, Elian moved stealthily towards an access grating set into the side of the tower, being careful not to be seen, and once more pulled out the Omni-gizmo.

'Does that thing have a laser cutter too, or something?' asked Julius, surprised. He had seen it in action the year before, aboard the Arneshian ship, a present from Valentina to Skye.

'It has pretty much everything you want,' said Elian, using the screwdriver function, to remove the grating. 'It's custom made, see?'

'I'll get you one for your birthday, McCoy,' said Faith. '*If* you get to celebrate another birthday that is ...'

'Thanks, mate.'

'Hold the grill and pull,' said Elian.

Julius grabbed hold of one end, with Faith at the other and, together, they began to pull at it. The grating popped off in a puff of dust.

Elian looked around anxiously to make sure that no one had detected them, then motioned for the boys to crawl inside the opening. Once they were in, she joined them, replacing the grid from within.

'I've found the terminal,' said Faith excitedly.

Julius stood up and moved on to join Faith. They were in a small rectangular area, where several crates were piled along its sides. There was just about enough space for the main frame and 5 or 6 people to stand. The grey, concrete walls rose to 60 feet above them, where they ended in a flat skylight.

'Can you find the blueprints for this camp on there?' asked Elian.

Faith began to shift items around on the terminal screen, his fingers moving fast. 'Here they are. It's much bigger than I thought.'

Julius examined the sprawling levels in dismay. Every one of them was as big as a city, large enough to contain roughly 4 million people.

'So, let's say we want to choose *this* spot here on the ground floor,' said Faith, lifting the com-link. 'We enter the co-ordinates in this self-teleporting thing, right? Like this ...'

'That's it, Faith,' said Elian. 'You've done it.' Her PIP vibrated just then, so she opened it up. 'It's JD,' she said, excitedly. 'Aurora here.'

'Elian!' said Kelly, obviously ecstatic to hear her voice. 'Are you all OK?'

'Yes. We've made it! We're inside the tower. What's going on up there?'

Kelly didn't answer straight away. 'The Arneshians have come out to play, but we're giving them a run for their money. Are you safe?'

'We are at the moment,' she answered.

'Captain, we have access to the backup terminal,' said Faith.

'There are more than a hundred subterranean levels here,' explained Elian. 'It's massive and the grounds are packed with guards. Plus, the airspace is choked.'

'Send me all you can, from that terminal,' said Kelly.

'Doing it right now, Captain,' said Faith.

'It looks like we're not going to be able to do what we did for Oceania. We don't have enough portals for that. I'll call a meeting with the GMs and the Curia right now, and we'll get back to you shortly. Stay put.'

'Roger that,' answered Elian, sounding miffed. She added a, 'Humph' for good measure at the end.

'He's just worried about you,' said Faith, trying to cheer her up.

'There was a time when he would have considered this situation his idea of a date, you know?' she said. 'Since he became Captain of the Mazda, his life has changed so much. *He* has changed so much.' She sat down on the dusty floor, and tried to get as comfy as she could. 'Then, of course, there's this issue with his dad.'

'Don't they get along at all?' asked Julius, eager for this opportunity to learn more about Kelly.

'They're really tight, but they just don't want to admit it. JD wants his approval but, for one reason or another, they always end up fighting. It's been like that since he graduated from the academy. That year, things really got messy. He argued with his dad and fought with his best friend — that's how he got that scar, by the way — until they both got locked in the brig for several days.'

'Wow,' said Julius. 'That bad, huh? What were they fighting about?'

Elian looked down, and started to play with her Omnigizmo. 'JD fell for his best friend's girl, and told him so. It ended in a brawl, with the girl in question breaking all ties with them both, until one of them gained some maturity. Eventually, they went their separate ways, both working hard for their posts. I guess in the end they *did* grow up.'

'Why did you choose Kelly?' asked Julius. 'I mean, *you're* that girl, aren't you?' Julius had seen how she had become enveloped in various multi-coloured wisps, something that wouldn't have happened if she were just telling a story about someone else. It had to be her.

Elian looked up at him, with a smile. 'He's my destiny,' she said, simply.

'If I were Morgana, I would have cried at this point,' said Faith.

'Mind you,' she added, 'it did take him the best part of fifteen years to ask me out. Faith, don't play with that comlink, please. It's very sensit–'

There was a puff of air, and Faith was gone in an instant.

'Faith!' cried Julius, groping at the space where he had been standing a moment earlier. 'Where did he go?'

'I think he just got teleported inside the compound,' Elian said, getting to her feet.

Julius' PIP vibrated and he answered it. 'Faith? Are you OK?'

'Yeah, but I think I gave a couple of folks here a heart attack. They're staring at me really weird-like.'

'Are there any guards in there?'

'They say no; just surveillance cameras.'

'Ask them where they're from?' said Elian.

There was silence for a couple of minutes, before Faith came back on the line. 'There's a mixture of people here. They say Canada, Peru, Illinois ... and various other places around there.'

'It's the Americas, then,' she said. 'OK, you need to find Ackley Smith. He's the Voice of the Earth for the Americas, but don't go below ground, to any of the lower levels, you hear? Send someone else to fetch him if you must.'

'All right, I'm on it, but don't you dare leave me behind again!'

'We'll come up with a plan, I promise,' said Julius. 'And I'll need your help.'

'Yeah, I've heard that one before,' he replied. Then Faith's voice became softer and slightly muffled as if he was covering his mouth. 'Make it quick, McCoy. Most of these folks look like you after that inorganic draw you did, three years ago. I'm not sure what's happening, but their energy levels are way low.'

Julius wasn't sure what to make of that comment, nor did Elian for that matter apparently, as she just shrugged her shoulders when he looked at her. He dismissed it from his thoughts, and started to examine the blueprints again, an idea forming in his mind. 'Now that Faith is inside there, do you think they can lock onto his com-link from the teleportation pads on Moonrising?'

'Why?' asked Elian.

'It's just an idea, but . . . can we try to contact Moonrising?'

Elian nodded and opened up a channel on her PIP. 'Moonrising, this is Aurora. Do you read me?'

'Go ahead, Aurora. Cress speaking.'

'We've infiltrated the ground level,' she said, winking at Julius.

'You were told to hold your position in the tower,' said Cress, sounding slightly agitated. 'Who's with you?'

'McCoy and Shanigan.'

'What?' spluttered Cress. 'Who ... How ... What is he ... What are they doing there?'

'There's no time for this, Nathan! I need you to listen to McCoy, please!'

'Put him on,' said Cress, still sounding rather shaken.

'Master Cress,' said Julius. 'Did you receive the data from Captain Kelly?'

'I did. What are you thinking?'

'The Arneshian fleet is busy with our Cougars, which leaves only the ground guards around the compound to take care of. There are only surveillance cameras inside, but no guards. If you can use the modified com-link as a receiver, and teleport several smaller versions of the portals into the room, then we can activate them from inside and people can just walk through them and hit the portal sequence, just like the Storks and Herons did with Oceania. There's too many of them for uplift — it would take forever. Am I making any sense?'

'One moment,' replied Cress. There were muffled voices on his end of the line, as Cress checked if what Julius had proposed was actually possible.

'He may be angry, but he's not stupid,' said Elian to Julius, quietly. 'If the plan is good, he'll go with it.'

Julius nodded, then decided it would be a good idea to contact Faith and update him on the plan. 'Mate, we need a clear way in. Can you get rid of the guards outside the main entrance?'

'There are plenty of people around me here nodding, and cracking their knuckles,' answered Faith. 'I think I'll have plenty of support.'

'Great. Tell someone to cover the cameras on that floor only. After that, get ready to receive a shipment of portals. You'll need to get folks to go through them. Do you understand?'

'Right. I'll try,' he said, sounding a little unsure. 'But, given how they reacted when I appeared out of thin air, I hope they're not thinking of burning me at the stake as a witch.'

'Cress says they'll do it,' said Elian suddenly, closing her PIP. 'Now all we have to do is actually get in there. Are you ready for some action, McCoy?'

'You bet. By the way, why did you tell him we were in there already?' asked Julius, as he removed the grating from the wall once more.

'What's done is done. We've given him one less thing to worry about, trust me.'

Julius couldn't argue with that. He paused in front of the opening and pulled his Gauntlet from his leg pocket, wearing it on his right hand. He turned to Elian. 'Listen, if these guards are anything like the others, they'll have some sort of device embedded in the palms of their hands, which they can use to attack with. They emit electricity ... or something like that, so watch out for them.'

Elian looked at him, intrigued.

'I found out last year,' he explained. 'T'Rogon's helpers – K'Ssander and A'Trid.'

'Thanks for the tip,' she said. 'I'll cover us, you do the shooting, OK?'

'Sounds good to me.'

As soon as they were outside, and out of the shadow of the tower, Elian activated her shields in a way that Julius had never seen before. She held her palms facing up, and streams of energy sprung into the air from them, like jets from a water fountain, which then fell around them, enveloping them in a protective cocoon.

'I feel like a hamster in a ball,' said Julius, admiring the sphere.

'It's a very special shield,' she said. 'You'll get one too, after graduation.'

They began to jog along the perimeter of the compound defence, Julius sticking close, just in front of Elian. Every now and then, she pointed her hands forward, whenever she needed the cocoon to stretch ahead of them, to give Julius some space. It had an appearance like a curtain of shimmering, thin cobwebs, constantly shifting about them in fluid movements.

'To the right!' called Elian suddenly, halting and reinforcing that portion of the shield.

Julius turned on the spot and saw a guard, holding his right arm towards them, looking quite startled. The man's palm was starting to glow, as if an internal neon light had been switched on inside it. He made a flicking gesture in their direction and a thin bolt of electricity shot out at them.

There was no hesitation from Julius, as he threw both of his hands forward, channeling a mind-push. Two single-bursts of golden energy shot out of the cocoon from Julius' Gauntlet. The Arneshian's electric bolt crashed harmlessly against the shield, and he flew backwards as he was lifted off the ground by the force of Julius' push, before crumpling in a heap a few feet away.

'Keep going!' called Julius.

Elian started to run. As they drew closer to the entrance, the number of guards increased considerably. It seemed that they had finally been alerted to the fact that there were intruders on the loose.

Julius noticed two of the Arneshians heading their way, open handed, ready to strike. He wasn't about to let them get any closer, and immediately fired off a volley from his Gauntlet which propelled them up and away. Instinctively, he whirled around and threw another blast in the direction of a guard that was trying to sneak up on them from behind.

'There's too many of them!' shouted Elian. 'What is that useless husband of mine doing?'

As if in answer to her question, two ferocious blasts shook the protective shield around the camp. Most of the guards stopped in their tracks, distracted by the new attack.

'Um, I hope our guys are remembering we're all still out here,' said Julius, nervously looking up to the sky.

'Actually they wouldn't,' said Elian, tensely. 'I told them we were inside, remember? Let's keep moving.'

From nowhere, two Herons came into view; they hovered in midair for a minute, before attempting to push through the shield. As they did this, the Arneshian guards, atop the towers surrounding the camp, targeted them. From below, it looked like an electric storm was raging high above, as waves of defensive strikes pummelled the Zed ships.

Julius saw that the cocoon of energy around him began to shift again, telling him that Elian was on the move. Being careful to remain inside its protection, Julius started to blast a path forward, occasionally throwing a burst of energy or a fireball to either side, whenever one of the Arneshians tried to flank them. He could see that the gate wasn't far off now, and there was something going on just outside, because there were Arneshians being lifted and dropped several feet away. As they got closer, he could see this was courtesy of Faith who was zipping left to right, up and down, deftly avoiding the guards' fire, and scattering them with mind-pushes.

Just then, Elian stumbled on a rock, and the shield clicked off as she fell.

Julius grabbed her by the arm, trying desperately to steady her. She slipped from his grasp and landed on the ground, but he at least succeeded in breaking the force of her fall. 'Get up. Get up!' he cried, aware of a group of Arneshians heading straight for them.

Elian scampered back up, but she wasn't quick enough to activate the shields again before the enemy got off several shots at them. Julius felt a sharp pain in his right shoulder, and he jerked sideways. It was followed by a burning sensation, which spread down his arm and up to his neck. There was no time to stop and check it out though so, grabbing Elian by her jumper, they ran the last few feet towards Faith and the entrance, while a barrage of electric energy bolts flew past their heads. Julius returned fire over his left shoulder, knowing that, even if he didn't actually manage to hit any of their assailants, at least he was making their life more difficult.

'Get back inside!' Elian shouted to Faith and the group of people helping him.

They stared at Elian for a second, not comprehending, then realised what was going on and dashed back through the door. As they reached the entrance, Julius pushed Elian inside first, then spun around, and projected a last burst of energy, which acted like a shockwave for five pursuing Arneshians, propelling them backwards into the air. He felt someone grab his jumper and pull him away, into the safety of the building.

'Quick, shut the doors!' shouted Faith.

Several people to either side of the entrance swung two vast wrought-iron doors closed. It momentarily struck Julius how odd that seemed, that they didn't have the automated doors he was so used to.

'That was close,' said Faith, shoving his back against the door.

'I never thought I would say this,' grunted a tall, dark haired man who, along with a host of burly men, was leaning against it too, 'but we *really* need to keep this shut and stay in here.'

'Julius,' called Elian, moving to the corner of the room. 'Help me with this furniture.'

Elian was standing in what looked like an impromptu office space. He saw a clump of metal desks and a group of large, heavy-looking filing cabinets scattered around the room, and understood immediately what she was looking to do. Quickly, the two of them began to lift the items with their minds, and shifted them towards the exit.

Faith, meanwhile, had turned to face the doors, and was using his own mind-skills to keep them closed, while his helpers edged out of the way as the furniture was stacked against the entrance. All this happened under the stares of a dozen or so other people, who looked scared, but also quite relieved that Zed had actually come.

'That should hold it for the moment,' said Elian. 'Besides, I think they have more pressing matters out there.'

'Hey Julius, you're bleeding, man,' said Faith, moving over to him.

Now that the adrenaline rush had passed, Julius remembered that he had been hit and, as he thought about it, his arm began to throb.

'Let me see that,' said Elian. 'Take off your jumper.'

Julius winced as he lifted his right arm to free it from the uniform.

'Hmm … nasty gash, but it looks worse than it is,' said Elian, examining it; a small stream of blood was trickling down his arm, but the wound was mostly cauterised, as it was singed around its edges. 'Come over here.' She led him to a nearby sink and carefully washed the excess blood away with cold water. Julius watched as it seeped down into the drain.

When she was happy that it was clean enough, Elian tore off a strip from the bottom of her t-shirt and ripped it in two. She wet one half, and used it to clean the wound as best as she could, then took the remaining strip and wrapped it around his arm, in a tight field-bandage. 'This will have to do for now.'

'Thanks,' said Julius, gently moving his arm.

'Let me through, y'all,' said a male voice, from the back of the small room. 'Please, let me through.'

Julius turned and saw a plump man, with sandy hair, probably in his mid-fifties, advancing towards them. He took Elian's right hand in both of his and shook it furiously. 'It's so good to see y'all! I'm Ackley Smith, Voice of the Earth for the Americas.' He kept Elian's hand tight, then he threw his arms around her and embraced her, swept up by emotion. 'I never thought I'd see this blue uniform ever again.' It seemed everything about Ackley Smith was expansive, including the healthy twang in his accent.

Julius just stood there, next to Faith, surprised, and slightly amused, by the reaction of this high status man, but fully appreciative of his feelings nonetheless. The room had gone quite, but he could hear a few sobs from somewhere in the midst of the small crowd gathered behind them. He also noticed how there were various threads of green and gold floating above their heads. The faces of these men and women, who had been so unceremoniously removed from their homes against their will, made Julius' heart ache. Some of them where wearing tattered dressing gowns, others dirty pyjamas — a sign that they had been abducted at dead of night. It was their sense of gratitude that he felt the most in that moment. Right then, Zed's existence, and importance made perfect sense to him. Being there, bringing hope back to these people, was what he had been trained to do, and it filled him with a welcome sense of satisfaction.

'Mr Smith,' said Elian, once he had let go of her, 'we have a plan for rescuing all of you, but I'm going to need your help.'

'Ah'll see to it,' he replied, promptly.

'How many people can we use to manage the crowds on each floor?'

'Everyone in this room has been in charge of maintaining control, since the start,' explained Smith. 'Each of them has also been in charge of others, on each floor. But, I have to warn you, the majority of folks in there don't look quite as … perky as we do.'

'What do you mean?' asked Elian.

'It's been that way ever since we got here,' said Smith, looking for confirmation from among his people, and receiving several nods in return. 'It's like people are tired or somethin', which is mighty strange because we've had food an' plenty sleep.'

'The people we rescued from Oceania were exactly the same,' said Faith.

'You found Oceania?' asked a man, barging to the front, excited.

'We did,' confirmed Julius. 'Just a few weeks back. They're all safe and back on Earth.'

'That's incredible!' said Smith. 'How did you do that? An entire continent?'

'It's a bit of a long story,' explained Elian, 'but we used the same technology the Arneshians used to bring you here. And we're about to do the same with all of you.'

'How long will it take?' asked Smith.

'Once the preparations are done,' said Julius, 'I'd say, just short of a month.'

'A *month*?' said an incredulous female voice from the crowd.

'I know it seems a long time,' said Elian, 'but these portals we're using to teleport you back home cannot cope with more than a million people per hour, and you have a lot of people here.'

Ackley Smith nodded in agreement. 'Ah'm not sure I fully understand how it all works, but it explains how this young man here,' he said, pointing at Faith, 'appeared out of nowhere, a while ago.'

'That's right; I used this device here,' said Faith, showing them the com-link.

'We want to use it to get some serious portals onto this floor,' explained Julius. 'All you'll have to do is walk through them and they'll take you back to Earth. It's perfectly safe, by the way.'

As Smith looked at the people behind him, checking for signs of approval, Julius could understand their doubts, but they really had no choice.

Smith turned to face Julius again. 'Tell us what you need.'

Cress had run Julius' idea by the technicians of Moonrising, which believed that it was a doable solution. The first thing they did, was to teleport into the compound a receiver larger than the link-com in Faith's possession, then a third one, larger than the previous one and so on, until the receiving platform was large enough to allow for the teleportation of the portals, which were roughly 40 inches high and 400 wide.

Once the first portal had been put into place, a small platoon of Zed officers appeared in the middle of the room, to everyone surprise. They were led by none other than Master Cress himself.

Elian and Ackley went to meet him, while half of the officers went to secure the exit door properly and the other half went towards the doors leading to the lower levels.

Julius noticed how visibly relieved Cress was to see that Elian was unharmed, before turning his attention to him and Faith.

'Master Cress,' began Julius, 'we're sorry, but it wasn't our fault! You have to believe us. The sky-jet malfunctioned and–'

'I'm aware of that, McCoy,' said Cress, nodding. 'It seems you have both redeemed yourselves from your previous foolishness. However, I still don't understand why you were on the Ahura Mazda to begin with.'

'They asked us to make a delivery, sir,' answered Faith, quickly.

'And you conveniently forgot that you were grounded on Tijara, did you?'

Julius was at least grateful that Cress wasn't shouting at them in front of everyone, but he was still getting rather tired of all this scolding business. However, he decided it would be wisest to keep his mouth shut for now, and avoid any further trouble.

'Get your things,' said Cress, looking at Julius' bandage. 'Grand Master Freja wants to see you, McCoy. And you, Mr Shanigan, will need to visit engineering.'

'Why?' asked Faith. Cress said nothing, and lowered his eyes. He followed the master's gaze, and saw that one of the bottom panels of his skirt was dangling loosely. 'Uh, right. I hadn't noticed that,' he said. 'So that's why I felt so ... tilted.'

'Come on,' said Elian, and escorted them to the portal. 'Thanks, boys. You really stood up for Zed today. I'll make sure I write that in my report.' As she said that, she glanced at Cress, and Julius got the distinct feeling that a mind-message had just passed between them. As if to confirm that, Cress looked down, a little smile formed briefly on his lips, before disappearing just as quickly.

Julius looked at the portal, and hesitated. All of the people in the room were observing with curiosity, waiting to see what happened when they walked through it. Cress strode over to Julius and Faith, placed his hands on their shoulders, and gently pushed them through, before following them. They were all gone in an instant.

Julius opened his eyes on Moonrising, checking that he was all in one piece. To his relief, he felt fine, as if he had simply done a hyperjump.

Cress led them towards Freja's office. When they arrived there, he said, 'McCoy, you wait here. Mr Shanigan, let's see to your skirt.'

Julius did as he was told. After grabbing a glass of water from the cooler in the corridor, he checked the time on his PIP, and was astonished to see that, in less than 30 minutes, it would be New Year. He wondered where Morgana was, and whether she knew what had happened. There hadn't been any ball organised this time, so it wasn't as if she would be at that. 'She's probably with Maks, anyway,' he thought. On impulse, he selected Farrah from his address book and typed her a message, ignoring the throbbing pain from his wound. "At Freja's office, about to get thrown out the air-lock, most likely. If not, I'll be spending New Year in the infirmary. Whoop-de-doo. Hope yours goes better. X"'

'Julius? What are you doing here?' It was Kelly.

Julius stood up. 'Freja wants to see me,' he answered, 'and I think that Cress is going to kill me this time.'

'Nah,' said Kelly. 'Once maybe, but he's calmed down a lot in recent years. He can be a hot head, but he's not stupid.'

'You seem to know him well, sir.'

'I do ... I did. He was my best friend at the academy, you see,' replied Kelly.

Julius almost choked on his water when he heard that. 'Wait till I tell the others,' he thought. So that surely meant that Elian had been Cress' girlfriend before, and therefore the cause of his friendship ending with Kelly. He had never really given much thought to Cress' private life. As his teacher, he was ... well, just Cress. He began to wonder then how many of the Tijaran staff had families, somewhere out there, waiting for them. Even Freja's had to have a family, it occurred to him.

Suddenly, the Grand Master's door opened and Freja stepped into the corridor. Upon seeing Kelly, his eyes widened in surprise. 'Captain Kelly?'

'Grand Master,' said Kelly, 'I need to speak to you.'

'Not now, I'm afraid,' replied Freja.

'Yes, now!'

Julius couldn't believe his ears. Had he really just heard Kelly ordering the GM to talk to him?

'McCoy needs to go to the infirmary, in case you hadn't noticed, before he passes out on your carpet.'

Freja instantly switched his attention to Julius. 'Are you wounded?'

'I don't think it's serious, sir,' he said, showing him the bandage under his t-shirt, which was now soaked in dark blood.

'Go, McCoy,' said Freja. 'We will speak at another time.' Then he turned to the Captain, coldness in his voice. 'Step into my office.'

Julius remained where he was as Kelly and Freja disappeared inside the room. As soon as the door had shut, Julius moved closer to it, eager to hear if Kelly would be decapitated for his insubordination.

'How could you have been so insensitive?' shouted Kelly.

'And how could *you* have been so selfish and reckless?' Freja cried back.

'Don't you dare accuse *me* of being selfish! If there's anyone here who tramples all over students' dreams, it's you! You've always cared more for this school than its pupils!'

'Don't give me that old story again. You should know better than that.'

'You always liked *him* better than me!'

'For the love of Tijara, John Dean ... don't be such a dramatic fool!'

'My name is JD.'

'I know that!' snapped Freja. 'I gave it to you!'

Julius was so shocked, he barely even noticed as the glass of water in his hand slipped from his grasp and landed with a thunk on the floor at his feet. *Freja's son ...*

'McCoy!' cried Kelly, from inside the room. 'To the infirmary! Now!'

Julius plucked the glass from the floor, plonked it down on a nearby coffee table, and ran down the corridor.

When he arrived at the infirmary, Nurse Primula was sitting behind the reception desk, beneath a row of colourful fairy lights, chatting with a colleague. When she saw him, she quickly stood and approached him, a look of concern on her face. 'What's happened to you?'

Julius, who was still mulling over the avalanche of news he had discovered about Kelly over the last 12 hours, snapped out of his reverie. 'Oh, I got hit by Arneshian fire.'

'Again?' she sighed, half-amused. 'Go to the usual room. I'll be right there.'

Julius made his way to the end of the foyer, beginning to feel quite tired and achy, and just a little lonely. It was about to toll midnight, and even Freja would have someone from his family to be with, even if that person was a "dramatic fool", as he had put it. Julius wondered where his parents were right now, and how they were spending the night. He imagined them huddled in each other's arms, in one of the Arneshian compounds, surrounded by countless strangers. He wished with all his heart that they were well, and nothing bad had happened to them. As for Michael, he had no idea where he could be, or with whom, even though he had a horrible feeling that he may be with Billy Somers.

It appeared that most of the infirmary beds were free at the moment; a situation Julius was sure would change as the rescue missions wore on. He entered the last room on the left, which was the one he used when he came for his Gene Therapy, and immediately dimmed the lights, inexplicably annoyed by their brightness. Gently, he removed his bloodied t-shirt and sat down on the bed, absently thinking that he would need to order a new jumper for his uniform.

Nurse Primula came in with a trolley and set to work at once. After removing the dirty bandage, she washed the cut properly. Next, she applied a disinfectant salve and held the Derma-Fix tool over the wound for a few seconds. Once it looked less inflamed, she prepared a new, waterproof bandage, containing a slow releasing healing paste, and wrapped it around his arm. 'There,' she said, standing up. 'Sorry you'll have to spend the night here, but tomorrow you'll be good as new.'

'Thanks.'

'Here,' she said, placing a pair of clean ward slacks on his bed. 'Shower's over there. You'll find towels and soap too.'

'A shower sounds great.'

'Well, happy New Year then,' she said, smiling.

'Let's hope so,' he replied.

Nurse Primula exited the room, leaving the door ajar.

Julius switched off the light completely and walked over to the window. He placed his left arm against the cold glass, and rested his forehead on it. From where he was, only stars and empty space were visible, no Cougars or Herons, and certainly no Arneshians. All was silent. Too many thoughts were passing through his mind, so he pushed them away. He would try to meditate a little to see if it helped him slee–

The light touch of small fingers stroking his shoulder blade, stopped his breath and sent shivers of goosebumps across his bare skin. Julius turned slowly, aware of how the hand hadn't moved away. He found Farrah's eyes looking back at him, close enough that he could see the stars reflected in them. She placed her other hand on his chest, gently, and Julius felt the muscles in his abdomen tensing, while a hot wave ran through his body. For a moment he was totally at a loss for words, the surprise of seeing her in the infirmary too big to handle. But it didn't last long.

It's now or never, he thought. He brought his hand up to her face, and lifted her chin towards him, all the while convinced that she must surely be able to feel his heart pounding wildly against her palm. Her lips glistened in the cold stellar light and, as they parted, her teeth shone like pearls. Julius ran his hand through her hair, to behind her head and gently pulled her closer, until his lips found hers. They kissed for a very long time.

CHAPTER 8

PRIORITIES

'Wake up, McCoy.'

The voice seemed to be coming closer, but Julius couldn't quite tell to whom it belonged. Not that he cared really, since he was presently lying on a beach, with the sun warming his skin. There was a tall coconut tree casting shade over his spot. When he looked at it, he saw that the initials "J & F" had been scratched into the bark; an empty green towel was laid out next to him, and he gazed towards the water, for any sign of her.

'Look at him. He's chasing rabbits.'

'Mmm ... gway ...' he mumbled, shooing the air, with a limp arm, desperately trying to cling onto the dream.

'Shake him,' said Skye.

'Oh, sweetie!' called Faith, shaking Julius, earthquake style.

"Nnnnn. Whasamatterwidya!' groaned Julius, waking up with a start, and looking, wide-eyed around the room. 'Where is she?'

Faith looked at Skye, puzzled. 'Where's *who*?'

'Hold it, hold it,' said Skye. 'Did you just say *she*? Was there a girl in this room last night?'

Julius stared at him, lost for words, as his brain tried to recall the events of the previous night.

'I don't believe it!' said Skye, grinning. 'Was it Farrah?'

'Farrah was here?' piped in Faith, looking around the room, as if he was expecting to find her hiding in the corner or something.

'Shhh!' said Julius, quickly. 'You want to get her into trouble?'

'You little, sly thing. Oh, come here you!' and with that, Skye leapt on Julius, and rubbed his knuckles against his head. 'You finally managed!'

'Did you kiss her?' asked Faith, eagerly. 'Did you?'

'Geroffme!' said Julius, half laughing and half attempting to shove Skye off his chest. 'What are you like?!'

'Congrats!' said Faith, making himself comfortable at the bottom of the bed. 'So?'

Skye let go of him. 'Come on, tell us all about it!'

Julius sat up straight, trying not to grin too much. 'There's not much to tell, you know.'

'Will you tell us, already?' said Faith, impatiently.

Julius duly obliged them, in the most gentlemanly terms that he could. When he finished, he slumped back against his pillow and drew a long sigh.

'That beats me New Year's Eve in engineering,' said Faith, disconsolately.

'I can't believe the nurses didn't see her,' said Skye. 'You lucky sod.'

'I know, right?' said Julius. 'What about you, Skye, where were you?'

'With this Irishman,' he answered, patting Faith on the shoulder. 'When I heard you were back, I came looking for you. They told me you would be spending the night in sick-bay, and that Faith was getting his skirt fixed, so I went to pester him.'

'He gave up Valentina for me,' said Faith. 'And I'm *much* hairier.'

'And Morgana?' asked Julius.

'She popped in to see us, with Maks,' said Skye. 'When we told her you were fine and stuck in here, she went back to New Satras.'

Julius nodded, pleased to know that she had at least tried to see him. 'I have some serious news for you both, by the way.'

'About what?' asked Faith.

'I have the perfect ending to the Kelly saga,' said Julius, smugly. 'But it'll have to wait till I get my breakfast.'

'OK, OK,' said Skye, standing up. 'Get dressed and meet us in the mess hall then. And don't take too long. The rescue mission is still ongoing, and they can call on us at any moment.'

'Roger,' said Julius, climbing out of bed. He lifted one corner of his bandage, and peered under it; seeing that the wound was dry, he took it off. A clean uniform had been placed on the chair next to the bed, and a pair of shiny boots had been left on the floor, probably by the nurse. He went off to shower, still very much unable to wipe the dreamy look off his face, wondering exactly how and when Farrah had managed to leave without being seen.

When Julius entered the mess hall, Morgana was sitting with Faith and Skye, eating her breakfast. He was glad to see her, and he also wanted to let her know that he too was now seeing someone, although he wasn't quite sure why. He grabbed some food from the counter and made his way over to their table. When he got there, the first thing he did was to wish her a belated happy birthday.

In reply, Morgana stood up and gave him a big hug. 'I'm so sorry, Julius,' she said, still holding him. 'I was mad at you when I left, and what if something had happened out there? I would never be able to forgive myself.'

Julius felt strangely unprepared to hear her apologies. He had been sure that she would still be cross about his behaviour, but obviously he had been wrong. 'I'm sorry too. I shouldn't have said those things.'

'That's sweet,' said Skye, vigorously chewing a rasher of bacon. 'And now, let's hear it.'

'They already told me about Kelly and Elian's marriage,' said Morgana, letting go of Julius and sitting down again. 'I'm so happy for them.'

'Guess who's not?' said Julius.

'We know that Kelly's dad doesn't know and wouldn't be too happy about it either,' said Faith. 'But *who* is he?'

Julius moved his head closer to the centre of the table; the others did likewise, and waited with bated breath. Julius gave it an extra couple of seconds for effect, then whispered, '*Freja* is Kelly's dad.'

'You're kidding, right?' said Skye, incredulous.

Faith and Morgana were staring at Julius in wide-eyed amazement.

'Everyone needs a dad, I guess,' said Julius.

'Wow,' said Faith. 'But Freja ...'

'Uh huh. I know, but don't even think about telling anyone else,' added Julius. 'Kelly and Freja know that *I* know, and if the story gets around, they'll be after me for sure.'

'Don't worry,' said Morgana. 'We'll not tell a soul.'

'Good. And did you tell them about Cress and Elian, Faith?'

'He did,' confirmed Skye. 'I never thought our master had the punch-up-for-love type of fight in him.'

'So *that's* how Kelly got the scar,' said Morgana, dreamily. 'That's so romantic. Has Kelly told Freja about the marriage?'

'I'm not sure. Maybe last night,' said Julius, shrugging his shoulders. 'He'll have to, eventually.'

'That'll sure make Cress cross,' said Faith. He winked, and added, 'See what I did there?'

'Yeah, shenanigans of Shanigan,' replied Julius, quick as a flash. 'See what I did there?'

Faith rolled his eyes and went back to his breakfast.

As far as the first of Januarys went, thought Julius as he tucked into his porridge, this one hadn't been too bad at all. While the others laughed and commented on Kelly's family tree, his mind was filled with images of Farrah. Even the mere thought of her made his stomach constrict, and the yearning to see her again soon even more painful. He found himself craving her kisses and longing to have her in his arms, so he could hold her tight and breathe in her scent. Honestly, was this normal or was he losing it? He wondered absently if it was maybe a little of both. He tried to focus on his food again, hoping that his feelings weren't too noticeable to the rest of the world. The real question though was, when would he next get to see her?

Even though Julius and Faith had contributed greatly to the Americas rescue mission, their ban from Satras hadn't been lifted, which they both found utterly unfair. As a result, Julius was limited to seeing Farrah by way of vidcall on his PIP, which wasn't nearly good enough, but it was all he had. Every free moment brought with it the perfect excuse to call, or text each other. Julius was getting well practiced at disguising these from the others although, to Skye's trained eye, it was all too clear what was going on.

Freja had still not summoned Julius to his office yet, which left him with a slight sense of dread hanging over his head. In fact, he hadn't seen him around the ship at all, and hadn't heard from Cress either. They were now a week into January and he was beginning to think that perhaps the Grand Master had forgotten about it.

Meanwhile, the mission was proceeding well, according to Professor Clavel. The Cougars and Herons were still stationed in the planet's orbit, to ensure that no Arneshians got back in. The guards patrolling the ground had all either been captured, or killed, during the fighting, but so too had some of the Zed officers. A ceremony was held in New Satras to commemorate the victims, with each of the coffins draped in a Zed flag. Not all of the bodies had been recovered, like those of the pilots who had died out in space; for each of them, a small urn was used, embellished with the Zed emblem, their names and ranks engraved on them. Julius and his classmates watched this on the TV in the mess hall, all of them deeply moved by the words that the GMs spoke. It was the first time they had witnessed a mass funeral in space and, when all of the coffins and urns had been ejected from the airlock, a few sobs were heard in the room.

Despite this, much to everyone's surprise, Zed met with very little resistance after that initial confrontation. Clavel told the Mizkis that, after losing their first foothold at the end of October, the Arneshians had been expected to focus their defences on the rest of the kidnapped Earthlings. Instead, all they had left to defend this new compound was a relatively small group of guards, which made everyone wonder what was *really* going on.

Mizki apprentices throughout Moonrising had been given a different task this time: that of compiling a massive database of all the people that had been rescued from Oceania. The Curia, who were particularly short on staff, had given them access to lists of names according to the latest Earth census, with the students being required to check each of the rescued earthling's names against this database. It was, without a doubt, the most boring job that Julius had ever done, but he realised how important it was to know that no one had been left behind, or was missing. Because he understood this, Julius continued to scan the database, day in and day out, hour after hour, without any complaint.

Even their classes had been cut down to a minimum, until their current assignment was completed, leaving just Clavel's and Chan's lessons to run as normal.

It was only in mid-January that Julius finally got the opportunity to leave the confinement of Tijara on an errand. To him though, what that *really* meant was a chance to see Farrah in person. Professor Turner was supervising the Mizkis as they went about their database chores, when she received a call. By chance, Julius was standing next to her desk, seeking help with a surname that he couldn't find.

'I can't right now,' she was saying to her earpiece. 'I won't be free for a few more hours, actually.'

Professor Turner listened for a moment, and her facial expression told Julius that no, whatever the caller wanted, it couldn't wait. She looked at Julius and raised an eyebrow, as if an idea had just popped into her head. 'I'm sending you one of my students: 4MA McCoy. Give it to him, please. Goodbye.'

'So,' said Julius, 'where am I going?'

I need you to head over to the Curia, by the main entrance. There's a package at reception which you need to bring back to me. Can you do that?'

'Of course,' said Julius. He was so eager to get out of Tijara for a while that he would have said yes to pretty much anything.

'Get there and get back quick as you can,' continued Turner. 'You're still grounded, so no excursions, understood?'

'Yes, Ma'am,' he said. He winked at the Skirts, got the thumbs-up from Skye and Faith, while Morgana limited herself to a small smile.

Julius took the corridor at a stride texting Farrah as he went, asking her to meet him by the Curia's entrance if she could, in five minutes.

'Please be there,' he murmured to himself, as he hopped on the lift to the fourth layer of the ship, which housed both the Curia and Moonrising's main hospital. A few moments later, as soon as the lift doors opened, he lunged out into the foyer, and scanned the ground for Farrah. He could see the main entrance and the reception desk beyond it; fortunately not many people were milling about. To the right of the Curia was a recess, partially hidden by a large, holographic hydrangea bush. Julius strolled towards it, trying to blend in as much as possible and, when he was sure that no one was looking, he dived into it. Once hidden from view, he poked his head back out, and scanned the area for Farrah. He saw her pop into view a few minutes later and a massive grin broke out on his face.

Farrah entered the large, well lit foyer, and nervously started scouting around for Julius. She walked past the entrance of the Curia and peered inside the glass doors, before moving on and stopping in front of the bush, twisting a corner of her jumper. Just as it looked like she was about to move again, a hand shot out from the hydrangea, grabbed her arm and pulled her through the bush. 'What–', she started.

'Shhh!' said Julius.

Farrah looked at him, and her eyes lit up. 'Julius! I've missed you so much!'

'So have I,' he said, the blood rushing to his face. He kissed her eagerly, wrapping his arms around her. Her body was pushed flush against his, as she passionately returned the kisses. Her scent called images of tropical, white beaches to his mind, while the taste of her strawberry balm melted in his mouth. He found himself wishing for that moment to last forever, as he revelled in feelings and emotions he had never experienced before. Right then, he didn't care that Professor Turner was waiting for him, or that she may be sending someone to look for her missing Mizki. He was ready to face a whole string of T'Rogons and Frejas, all mixed together, with Cress on top and Foster for dessert, rather than let Farrah go.

'Ahem,' said a voice from the other side of the bush, suddenly.

Julius and Farrah froze, lips still glued together.

'I'm sure I haven't just seen two students kissing in the bushes,' said the voice. 'How could I? Students couldn't possibly be in there. I must be tired.'

'Mr Hastings?' called Julius, afraid to let him see Farrah.

'Mr McCoy? How's the hydrangea today?'

'I'll call you later,' Julius whispered to Farrah.

'You better,' she said seductively in his ear, before planting a light kiss on the tip of his nose.

Julius got lost in her eyes for a moment, then let her sneak away through the back before he moved. Straightening his uniform, he stepped out of the bush.

Ben Hastings was standing there, arms crossed and head cocked to one side. 'I must have missed the briefing,' he said, sounding amused. 'Do active duties now extend to gardening?'

Julius flattened his hair, and looked down, sheepishly.

Hastings laughed, obviously enjoying the situation. 'I take it that's your girl, then?'

Julius nodded, still feeling quite embarrassed, but pleased to be able to answer yes to that particular question. 'I hadn't seen her for a while,' he began to explain.

'Don't worry about it,' said Hastings, waving his hand. 'But you need to be more careful in the future. And why here, of all places?'

'Actually, I'm supposed to pick up a package for one of my teachers,' he said pointing at the main entrance to the Curia.

'Well, you best go do that then,' said Hastings. 'I'll wait for you.'

Julius nodded and hurried away.

As he entered the building, the stout, bald man at reception looked up from his desk. 'Are you McCoy?'

'Yes, sir,' replied Julius, bowing.

'Retinal scan, please,' he said, lifting a hand in front of him. 'Look at my palm.'

The centre of the man's hand glowed brightly as Julius looked at it, and there was a beep, followed by a green light. 'We have to be careful,' the man said, then grabbed a small parcel from under the desk and handed it to Julius.

Once outside, Julius walked over to Hastings.

'Let me escort you to the lift,' the Curiate said. 'In case you should get lost again.'

Julius grinned, thankful that Hastings was being so relaxed about it; not so much for himself, but for Farrah.

'I heard about your latest adventure, in the Americas compound,' said Ben. 'That was well done. Risky, but well done.'

'It was Lieutenant Elian Flywheel who took the initiative, actually.'

'So I've heard. Still, you and Mr Shanigan played your part well, so don't be modest and take a bow.'

'Thank you, sir,' replied Julius, pleased that at least someone was able to see that he wasn't just being reckless.

'I take it you're still banned from New Satras, yes?'

'Hence the hydrangea,' sighed Julius.

'Well, you're not the first student to think of that,' said Hastings, chuckling. 'Don't worry though, the ban will be lifted soon.'

'Really?' said Julius, stopping. 'How do you know?'

'A benefit of my job. The Curia does have *some* powers over the schools, you know?' replied Hastings, knowingly.

'That's a serious piece of good news, sir.'

'Don't go tiring yourself out though, McCoy. You look tired enough as it is.'

'Everyone is, I think,' replied Julius, starting to walk again. 'We're all doing our part.'

'Sure, I know, but ...' Hastings looked at him, with concern. 'Listen, I can't really say too much, but you really should rest whenever you can. When you get back to New Satras, try not to overdo the games, or the dating.'

Julius wondered what he meant by that and why he was being so insistent about the R&R. Then he remembered the classified file he had found in Cress' office, and it dawned on him that Ben Hastings may have more information than he did. He needed to find out if this was the case. 'Sir, since you seem to have a good opinion of me and my abilities as a Mizki, would it be too much to ask for a little more information? I won't tell anybody, I promise.'

Hastings looked at him seriously. 'We — the Curia, that is — know that Freja has his eyes on you for a *very* important mission.'

This, Julius knew already. He wondered if he should tell Ben about the file. Hastings had been cool about covering up for him and Farrah, but what would he do if he knew of Julius' breaking-and-entering activities? He was still a Curiate, after all, with his own responsibilities. Perhaps it would be best to fake ignorance and let him talk. 'A mission?' he said, trying to sound surprised.

'Think about all you've been through as a White Child already,' continued Ben. 'Freja has allowed you to do more than a lot, for a Mizki. Not forgetting your special DNA augmentations over the past two years. His plans for you are *big*.'

Julius had read all of this in the file. He decided to change tactic. 'Sir, should I be worried?'

Hastings shifted his weight from one foot to the other, looking suddenly uneasy. 'Freja's a clever man. He always has been. I'd be careful if I were you. Sometimes I think that he loves his school more than his students.'

Julius had heard that before, coming from none other than the GM's own son, Captain Kelly. But what did it all mean for Julius? Would Freja *really* send him on a one-way mission? Suddenly, the joy he had felt with Farrah just a few minutes earlier was gone, replaced by a growing sense of anxiety. As they approached the lift, he stopped and bowed to the Curiate. 'Thanks for the heads-up, Mr Hastings,' he said. 'I'll keep my strength.'

'You do that, McCoy,' replied Ben. Then he opened his PIP and typed something quickly. 'I've just sent you my direct number. Call me if you need.'

'Thank you, sir' said Julius, and stepped into the lift.

The mission continued throughout that month, until it was brought to a successful end on Wednesday the 22nd of January. After the last million Earthlings had been rescued, the Americas' compound was blasted off the face of the planet by the Zed fleet, and its destruction was broadcasted on all of Moonrising's screens. Iryana Mielowa was, of course, there to give a detailed account of all the proceedings, with live interviews from the three hangars of the schools. It was the second cause for celebration they had had since leaving the Lunar Perimeter, and everyone gathered to toast the occasion, some in New Satras and others in the schools' mess halls.

Julius chatted to Farrah pretty much all of that night, and couldn't refrain from telling her that his ban would soon be over. He didn't mention his talk with Ben about Freja's plans for him: their time together was already so short that he didn't want to worry her needlessly.

Julius however, had underestimated the true level of his anxiety about this whole secret mission business because, as the last weekend of January passed him by, he began to feel increasingly nervous and heavy-hearted.

Unknown to him, his downcast mood did not escape some of his friends and, on Sunday, after lunch, he received a message from Morgana: "Meet me in room H2B, Training Area, 3PM. M."

Julius wondered what she could want as he hadn't seen her all weekend. When the time came he made his way towards the south end of Tijara. He could tell from the name of the room that it was a holographic class on the second level. He went down the stairs and along the corridor, until he reached the door. 'Computer, activate 4MA Ruthier,' he said. Then pressed the entry button, and walked in.

Morgana had activated a countryside programme, which didn't surprise Julius in the least. Whenever she had been feeling troubled about something, or needed peace, she always went back to nature. The afternoon sun was shining warm and bright over lush, green pastures. Julius took his jumper off and left it on the ground by the entrance, which was hidden behind a large boulder. He could hear the bleating of sheep in the distance, rolling towards him from beyond one of the small hills. The landscape reminded him a lot of the Scottish Borders back home, but he couldn't tell for sure if that was what the holographic setting had been modelled after. He took a few steps, looking around; then he spotted Morgana sitting beside a stream, her silhouette dark against the sunlight, and made his way over there.

'Hi,' he said, as he reached her.

Morgana looked up at him, and smiled. She had taken her boots off and had her feet in the water. 'Thanks for coming. Join me.'

Julius sat down, took his own boots off, and rolled his trousers up to his knees, before dipping his feet into the water. It was cool, and he immediately felt refreshed by it. He threw a glance sideways and saw that Morgana had her head tilted back, as she basked in the sun's glow. Her dark hair was alight with sparkling reflections that flitted about as the breeze rippled through it. For a moment, he thought about the dance they had had, the previous year when, for the first time, he had looked at her like a boyfriend might, rather than just a friend. He shook the thought from his mind, as a feeling of guilt crept into his consciousness, given that he was with Farrah now.

'I know we haven't spoken much, lately,' said Morgana, not noticing his passing moment of discomfort. 'I've missed you.'

Julius wasn't sure what to reply to that.

'You weren't there for my birthday, for the first time since we've met. Times change, I guess.'

There was no blame in her words, Julius felt, just a hint of sadness.

'So, how's things?' she asked, more lightly. 'You seem happy with Farrah.'

'I am,' he said. 'You'd like her.'

Morgana nodded. 'We should all go out, for sure.'

'Skye wants to organise a dinner or something, so we just need to get Siena and Faith to team up.'

'He'll need some *serious* help,' said Morgana.

Julius could sense the tension easing a little. Despite that, and as much as he was happy to just chat with her like this, he was also quite curious as to why she had invited him here. 'So, what did you want to talk to me about?'

'You,' she answered, simply. 'Lately you've seemed a little on edge, and tired, like there's something on your mind that you don't want to share with any of us.'

'Did the guys ask you to come speak to me?'

'No. It was just me, actually. I can always tell when you're stressed. So I decided to meet you. Was that wrong of me?'

'No, of course not,' he said, wondering how much he should tell her.

'Look,' continued Morgana, 'I don't care what you do in your spare time, Julius, because you're old enough to decide that for yourself. But I'm your friend, even if we haven't seen each other much lately. And, unless you tell me not to be your friend anymore, I'll always be here for you.'

'You'll *always* be my friend; don't be silly,' he said, surprised that she would even think something like that. 'It's just that ... you're right, I *am* stressed.' Morgana was listening intently now, and that encouraged him to go ahead. 'I feel under pressure. My head is cluttered and, no matter how much I try, I can't seem to sort it out.'

'What's burdening you?'

'*Everything*,' he said, relieved at finally being able to let go of some of his cares. 'I worry about Mum and Dad. I think about Michael spending time with Billy Somers. I wonder how long the rescue missions will continue for, or this stupid ban, for that matter. And, on top of all this, there's that classified file business and that mission they have in stock for me.'

'I wouldn't stress over that one,' she said. 'You don't even know if Freja would actually ask you to do it.'

'But I *do*,' he replied. 'One of the Curiates, Ben Hastings, told me that Freja has plans for me.'

'A Curiate? When?'

Julius told her about Hastings and all of their past meetings, ending with the latest one, in which he had recommended that he take it easy.

Morgana was silent, and thoughtfully smoothed the creases in her skirt.

'What is it?' Julius asked her.

'Nothing ... except, why would a Curiate give you the heads-up on a classified mission before the GM? It's a bit unprofessional, don't you think?'

'It's probably because I pushed him to find out. That, and the fact that he likes me, I guess. Anyway, it's not an issue.'

Morgana didn't seem too convinced, but let it go.

'So, how do I declutter my head, then?' he asked. 'You're the expert on this stuff.'

'I think you need to get your priorities right,' she said, lightly splashing the surface of the water with her feet. 'Most of the worries you mentioned are outside of your control, Julius, and there's nothing you can do to change them at this point in time. You need to let them go.'

'What am I left with, then?'

'Yourself, and what you can become if you focus on that.'

'What do you mean?'

'I mean that your concern should be for the development of your true nature to its full potential. You were born a White Child for a reason, and you have a duty to yourself not to waste that gift. And not because *others* want you to, but because *you* want to.'

'Ben told me the same thing,' said Julius, quietly. 'He said that I should use this gift to bring hope back to people.'

Morgana rummaged through her bag and pulled out a card. 'Here,' she said, handing it to him. 'Early birthday present.'

Julius took it, puzzled. On the cover was the picture of a dragonfly, its vivid blue and black colours in stark contrast to the paleness of the water.

'It symbolises victory in Japan,' she explained. 'Open it.'

He did so and read the inscription.

"If you can't choose the song,
You'll have to learn to dance to the music that's playing."

Julius felt a fleeting heartache as he read the words and realised how well she knew him. The words may not have been the same as his own personal maxim, but the meaning was: adapt and survive.

Morgana lifted her feet out of the water and stood up. She picked up her boots and socks, but didn't move. 'What are you *really* afraid of, Julius?'

'What?' he replied, startled. 'I'm not afraid of anything. I'm just worried, that's all.'

'You've been in dire straits before, and you came through it without breaking a sweat. What's different this time?'

Julius shook his head. 'I don't know what you want me to say.'

'What is your fear?'

'I don't know.'

'Then you'll need to find out.'

Julius spent the next few days thinking about his talk with Morgana. He had placed the dragonfly card on his bedside table, and would stare at it, as he recalled their meeting. Her words had deeply troubled him, and he couldn't quite understand the reason why that was. He kept asking himself about what his biggest fear was, but somehow the answer seemed to elude him, as if, subconsciously, he didn't want to find it. She had been right about the fact that he was worrying too much, about many things that he couldn't change, but he wasn't doing it on purpose.

Faith and Skye had asked him if he was all right on a couple of occasions, when he got lost in himself, to which he simply replied that he was tired. He avoided telling Farrah anything too, and had to use the same excuse with her, only she wasn't really buying it, and told him as much. Still, she didn't press him into telling her either, for which Julius was immensely grateful.

On Thursday 31st January, the 4MAs were working with Professor Turner, updating the Americas database, starting with Mexico. Since that was Manuel Valdez's home country, he had prepared a personal list of family and friends, which he had sent to his classmates, asking them to prioritise it, if it wasn't too much trouble. Occasionally the silence was broken by a spontaneous expression of joy, whenever one of the Mizkis spotted one of the names from the list; each time this happened, Manuel would run up to them to see who it was. Julius could have sworn that he saw his eyes welling up a few times and definitely once, when he saw his mom and dad's names.

Around 16:30, Professor Turner approached Julius' station. 'The Grand Master would like to see you, McCoy.'

'Thank you, Professor,' replied Julius. He turned to the Skirts, and grinned. 'Fingers crossed, guys, but it looks like my detention may be over.'

'In that case, don't forget about me,' added Faith. 'I'm sick and tired of being confined to this ship.'

'I won't,' he said, standing and darting out of the room.

When he arrived at Freja's office, he paused to allow his breathing to calm a little, then straightened his uniform and knocked on the door. It slid open and Julius stepped into the GM's office.

Freja was sitting at his desk and bowed his head to Julius as he entered. 'Please, sit,' said Freja, indicating the chair opposite him.

'Good evening, sir,' said Julius, sitting.

'I was meant to meet with you earlier in the month,' began Freja, 'but it has been rather hectic. How are you? I take it your wound wasn't serious?'

'Oh no. Ms Primula took care of that, sir.'

'Very well,' he said. After looking at Julius for a few moments, he said, 'Aren't you going to ask me about Captain Kelly?'

Julius was taken aback, but then again, Freja did know that *he* knew. 'It *was* a surprise, sir. I guess a student never imagines that everyone has family, even teachers.'

Freja nodded, and smiled. 'JD took his mother's surname. He said he'd rather keep his family tree hidden. He was never one for favouritism.'

'You have a great son, sir. I owe him a lot, already. I haven't spoken about his family with anybody ... well, except the Skirts that is. They were with me when Captain Kelly and Lieutenant Flywheel were discussing their ....'

'Thank you, McCoy. I know now. We appreciate your discretion.'

Julius nodded, all the time wondering when Freja would get around to his ban. Instead, the GM asked him an unexpected question.

'I can imagine you've been under a lot of stress, lately. I hope your friends have helped take your mind off things. Perhaps a girlfriend, even?'

Julius did his best not to betray his surprise. Was Freja really asking about his love life? Suddenly, the image of his classified file sprung to mind, with that note at the end of the page about FH; just in case it really was referring to Farrah, Julius decided to lie about it. He couldn't risk being banned from seeing her. 'No time for girls, sir,' he said. 'You keep us far too busy for that.'

'Mr Miller seems to manage,' answered Freja.

'He's a particular case, as you probably know.'

Freja laughed. 'I believe I've heard,' he said. He studied Julius for a moment, then changed topic. 'I read Lieutenant Flywheel's report. You did well, McCoy. You and Mr Shanigan.'

'Thank you, sir,' he said, relieved and surprised that Freja wasn't still mad at him, for leaving Tijara.

'It was a good piece of improvisation, that kick started our mission without any further delays. I won't hide the fact that we were very worried when we heard but ... well, it's done now. And their opposition was minimal enough to pose no real threat to us.'

'About that, sir,' blurted out Julius, before he could stop himself.

'Yes?'

Seeing as Freja seemed inclined to listen, he went on. 'There's something *off* about their lack of defence. And about the lack of Nuarns, for that matter. I thought perhaps you knew why.'

'As a future captain of the fleet, I would hope you'd have your own answer for that.'

'Ideas, mainly,' he replied, tentatively.

'Try me.'

Julius thought about it, then said, 'Well, why go to all the bother of kidnapping the humans, just to give them back so easily, continent by continent and unharmed? Not that I'm unhappy about that, of course, but it feels ... staged.'

'In what way?'

'Like we're being led from A to B, just to keep us busy. And never mind how we *found* A in the first place.'

Freja nodded. 'It did occur to us as well, I must say. So, what about the Nuarns?'

'T'Rogon said before that they had enough of them to last a lifetime of experiments.'

'That tape was a fake, remember? There's no proof that they're being harmed in any way.'

'Then where are they, sir?'

'There's only one place left that we know of,' said Freja.

'Arnesh?' wondered Julius aloud.

'Why not? It's their stronghold after all. Their entire defence system is sure to be there.'

Julius mulled it over, weighing up the likelihood of Freja's guess. As he thought about it, his eyes wandered to the Arneshian artifact, which was lying on a stand on the Grand Master's desk, and grew wider as he noticed something.

Freja followed his gaze. 'What is it?'

'Two of the sections are switched off now,' said Julius. He stood up and moved closer to the object. 'It was only one when I first found it.' He turned to the GM. 'When did this happen?'

'Last week, after we completed the Americas mission,' answered Freja, watching Julius. 'Any theories as to how and why?'

Julius carefully studied the silver object. The four arms all branched out into two symmetrical portions at the end of each one: a small sphere with three short arms, each ending in a little square. Both portions of one of the arms were now turned off. 'I think that they represent two of the five continents. Oceania and the Americas are the smallest in population, since the Chemical Wars, so they're are both at the end of the same arm,' explained Julius. 'The rest of the arms are for the remaining, largest continents.'

Freja nodded. 'Go on.'

Julius picked up the artifact, and ran his fingers along the length of the four arms, feeling all of the holes as he did so. Suddenly, he caught sight of something glinting on the floor and, without thinking, he moved the artifact until one of the holes was right above it, which allowed him to see that it was clearly a loose screw. An idea formed in his mind and he looked up at Freja.

The GM sat up straight, intrigued by Julius' reaction.

'I don't know what each of these squares, spheres and triangles mean, exactly, or what they stand for,' began Julius, 'but the only other idea I can think of, is that this artifact is actually a guide. Grand Master, do we have a star-map that shows the exact locations of the first two missions?'

Freja nodded and activated his desk. He quickly found what he was looking for and, plucking the virtual map by its corners with the tips of his fingers, he stretched it out so that it covered the entire length of his desk.

Julius passed the silver object to him. 'Can you align the planets where we found Oceania and the Americas with the two holes on the lit off arm, in such a way that-'

'...all the other holes are filled with a planet ...' finished Freja, excitedly.

Julius watched as he moved the artifact over the desk, not even aware that he was holding his breath.

Freja adjusted its position a few times, and the size of the map, to ensure that the two planets they had already visited would remain visible through the holes. Once he was happy, he placed the object flat on the map and dimmed the main light. 'Look,' he said.

Julius stepped over to the desk and examined it from above. The room was bathed in eerie blue light, emanating from the map and the artifact. Each of the holes was now filled with a bright dot, which represented a planet. 'We have no knowledge of these new systems. Still, thank you, Julius,' said Freja. 'If you're right, our people won't be waiting long.'

Julius nodded, unable to answer, on account of the knot in his throat; he knew that one of those dots was sure to be a planet which held the citizens of Europe, where his mum and dad would be waiting to be rescued.

Freja didn't switch the lights back on, but instead sat down on his chair, his face looking thoughtful. 'You can tell Mr Shanigan that your ban is lifted. And now, if you'll excuse me, I have three missions to plan.'

'Yes, sir!' said Julius, thrilled by this news. He bowed to the GM and hurried out of the room. He checked his PIP and saw a message from Faith, saying that they were all in one of the booths in the mess hall. Julius started to jog: he was eager to tell his friends all about his discovery and, after that, he would dash to New Satras to give Farrah the good news, in person.

CHAPTER 9

BEFORE THE STORM

After the lifting of the ban, Julius and Faith were finally able to spend more time in New Satras with the rest of the Skirts. The group had naturally expanded to include the respective love interests, much to everyone's satisfaction. As well as Maks and Valentina, Farrah was now also a fixed feature. Although they weren't actually going out, Siena and Faith were simply considered the fourth couple; everyone, except perhaps for Faith, knew that it was only a matter of time before they hooked up. As well as "couple time", many of their free afternoons and weekends were spent in group activities, whether that was in a sim-room, or in one of New Satras' many cafes.

It was a new experience for the Skirts, a new phase of life, which Julius liked very much. Having Farrah by his side, her head resting on his shoulder, was not an issue and did not make him feel embarrassed, especially because everyone else was doing much the same. Julius found fascinating watching Siena trying to get closer to Faith, doing things like casually leaving her hands where he could find them but, inevitably, Faith never picked up on it. Whether this was down to him simply not noticing, or because he was pulling one of his nervous, inept-at-dating stunts, was unclear, however, it was agreed that they really needed to help him out before Siena decided that it was no longer worth it.

One Saturday afternoon, near the end of February, Julius, Morgana, Skye and Siena were having lunch at Eat Your Mama Blind. They had worked hard all week finishing the database for the Americas, and were now reaping the satisfaction of a job well done. The Mizkis had been told that while Moonrising was preparing for the next mission, all students would return to a more-or-less regular timetable, with most of their classes opening up once more.

'I think we should organise a proper meal soon,' said Skye, stretching in his chair. 'We've worked hard and I bet we could find a few reasons to gussy up.'

'I'd like that,' said Morgana. 'One fancy dinner to make up for the lost New Year's ball, missed birthdays and, of course, to celebrate the successful missions.'

'I wish *I* had something to celebrate too,' said Siena, sulking.

'Awww,' said Morgana, hugging her. 'He's such a silly, isn't he? I bet he thinks about you all day, and he doesn't know how to tell you.'

'Speaking of ...' said Julius, pointing out the window.

Zooming in and out of the crowd, Faith was on his way to the restaurant, looking slightly crazy. Julius was immediately worried and leapt up from his chair, hurrying to the entrance. A second later, Faith crashed through the doors, straight into Julius' arms, and dragged him back to the table.

'What's the matter?' asked Morgana. 'Is everything OK?'

Faith, it seemed, was unable to talk properly, but he was grinning, which at least put the others at ease.

'What is it?' pleaded Julius, growing ever more curious.

A soft whisper of a reply escaped Faith's mouth, which they all had to lean in close to hear. 'I did it. I won Pete's spaceship design competition!'

'Awesome!' exclaimed Julius. 'I'm so proud of you, mate!'

'Congrats!' cried Skye, patting him on the back.

'Well done!' said Morgana, hugging him tight. 'I knew you could win it!'

'Cheers. It was tough, though,' said Faith. 'The other competitors were all older than me. I knew I had to come up with something really special to beat them.'

'So what did you do then?' asked Skye.

'I created a couple of things. One is a new engine, to help make longer jumps,' he explained. 'Pete said he wants to call it the Shanigan's Relay.'

'That is amazing,' said Morgana, awestruck. 'And what was the other thing?'

'A space coffin,' said Faith, a little more tentatively.

'A what?' asked Skye, 'Why?'

'Well, it's just that when we release one of our people into space, I always wonder what happens to them — you know, how long their bodies will look nice for, or their coffins will last and the like. Everyone deserves a proper rest … afterwards.'

'You're so thoughtful, Faith,' said Morgana. 'I think it's a splendid idea.'

'Are they really going to build your inventions?' asked Siena, excitedly.

'Absolutely,' answered Faith. 'Although, they might have to do it a little bit here and a little bit there, with the missions taking top priority and what-not.'

'Oh, Faith,' said Siena, smiling proudly, but still seemingly too shy to move any closer.

'There!' said Julius. 'Now, we have the perfect excuse for that fancy dinner!'

'You've got that right!' agreed Morgana, standing and picking her things up from the chair. 'I'm gonna go see Maks and find out when he's free.' She hugged Faith again. 'You and your magnificent brain!'

As she left, Faith slumped down into a chair, exhausted, but clearly over-the-moon. 'So, what's this dinner thing?'

'It will be a great night,' said Skye. 'A celebration of all the good things that have happened this year. It's for the Skirts only, and their partners.'

'Or whoever you'd like to invite,' added Julius, hinting at Siena with his head.

Faith stared at Julius for a moment, studying his head movements, mystified. Thankfully, it dawned on him to look in the right direction and, when he saw Siena, he grinned. Casually, he turned to her and said loudly, 'Well, paint me brown and call me a turd!' followed by a cheeky wink.

A moment of stunned silence descended on the table, while Siena stared at him, in disbelief. After a brief, uncomfortable few seconds, she snapped her head in the other direction and stormed out of the restaurant.

Julius and Skye watched as she left, and then turned back to Faith, incredulous.

'Really, Faith? Really?' groaned Julius. 'A turd?'

'For the love of Zed!' cried Skye. 'What possessed you to say something like that?'

'Why?' asked Faith, sounding genuinely puzzled. 'What did I say?'

'Come with me,' growled Skye. He grabbed Faith by the arm and dragged him outside.

Julius, eager not to miss any of this, hurried after them.

'Where are we going?' said Faith.

'Shut up and hover,' replied Skye, fuming.

When they reached the holographic sector, Skye selected the sim-dating programme and turned to Faith. 'It's time you use that voucher we gave you for your birthday. I don't care how you do it, or how long it takes, but this will be your home until that meal. I'll get you two together if it's the last thing I do, or my name isn't Black-Hole Miller. Am I clear?'

'Yeah, sure thing, buddy,' said Faith, nodding and looking slightly frightened.

'Good. Get in there!' He nodded to Julius. 'I'll see you later, McCoy.'

Julius watched as they disappeared inside the room, and burst out laughing. He was still chuckling when he got back to Farrah and was unable to stop, even after he had told her the story a couple of times.

Once he had himself under control again, they decided to forget Faith's lady troubles for a while and found a nice, quiet, very isolated corner where they could spend the next few hours in peace.

As March got underway, Julius' mood had lifted slightly, thanks mainly to the thought that if the artifact really was a map, they would soon be able to locate another continent. With the regular classes underway, a sense of normality had returned to the students, bringing a feeling of spring to their hearts.

Julius continued to enjoy his Twist lessons, and it didn't take long for him to improve his rebinding of molecules to a satisfactory level. While most of his classmates were still tackling small objects, Morales had moved Julius to one side of the room and given him bigger and more complicated things to twist; everything from engine cores to Sky-jets. Whenever he grew bored of those, he turned his attention to other, more interesting objects, such as the classroom door, whenever Morales wasn't looking. The resulting laughs from the Mizkis would prompt her to turn around, but Julius had become a fast hand and was able to rebind it before she could catch him out. Eventually though, he had to stop this when, one day, an unaware student on his way out to the toilet, almost got trapped inside the very fabric of the door, scaring them both almost to death.

In Telekinesis class, Professor King continued his obstacle course training, where students practiced moving each other along it, using their mind-skills. Faith had been very careful never to pair up with Siena, just in case he accidentally dropped her in front of everyone and really killed his chances with her. Skye and Julius agreed that it was probably the sensible thing to do.

It took a lot of back-and-forth before the Skirts were able to find a date for the meal that suited everyone; eventually, it was decided that it would take place on Saturday the 23rd of March, in one of the holographic rooms in New Satras. Then began the problem of deciding the virtual setting and, as everyone had completely different ideas on the matter, they resorted to a lucky draw, where the chosen person would be the one calling the shots.

To her delight, Farrah won. She hopped up and down several times, clapping her hands happily. 'I'll send the invitations out soon!'

A few days later, all the guests received a little parcel in the mail. Julius opened his with Morgana and Siena, in the lounge.

'Oh my,' said Morgana. 'It's a shell!' She held it up for the others to see, delicately touching the shiny inner surface.

'Mine is a piece of red coral,' said Siena, admiring it. 'What do you have, Julius?'

Julius opened the small envelope, and a stream of white, fine sand ran out into his cupped hand. 'I get the feeling that we're going somewhere tropical,' he said, rubbing the sand between his fingertips. It reminded him of the dream he had had on the night when they had first kissed, and was amazed at the coincidence.

'Where did she get these things?' wondered Morgana.

'Her folks have a shop of old Earth stuff on level -2,' explained Julius.

'That's right. I've seen it!' said Siena. 'Auld Oddities, yeah?'

'That's the one,' answered Julius.

'Dress code is smart-casual,' read Morgana, from her invite. She looked at Siena. 'We need to check out some pictures of people at beach parties and see what kind of things the guests wear.'

'Absolutely,' said Siena.

'I seem to remember white being a prominent colour,' added Morgana helpfully.

'You're right!' agreed Siena. 'Also, linen is a good material for the clothes.'

'It does crease a lot though,' said Morgana, sounding almost crestfallen.

Julius stared blankly at the pair of them. 'I'm gonna leave that particular search to your good selves. Just tell me what to wear and I'll do it.'

'Let's go see Farrah,' said Siena. 'We should help her out with the preparations!'

As it turned out, the Skirts had chosen the best possible time to celebrate since, a few days later, it was announced that a new continent had been located and that the third mission would began on Monday the 25th of March. Judging by the number of bio-signatures present, they believed it was Africa. The excitement spread through Moonrising like wildfire, tempered slightly by the frustration of those who still had missing relatives and friends from the remaining, unfound two continents.

To his great surprise, Julius received a short message from Freja that read, "It is a map! Well done." Feeling quite pleased with himself, he showed it to the others and, of course, to Farrah, although he couldn't help telling her a slightly more colourful version of the story; how he had discovered the true nature of the artifact, preventing Freja from making a fatal mistake that could have led Moonrising off course by several light years. Farrah listened intently to him, enraptured, before hugging him tight and showering him with kisses.

Julius had come to associate his time with Farrah as the only time in which he could truly relax, leaving his anxiety behind. She had that effect on him, and he couldn't imagine ever letting her go. These feelings both astonished and excited him, and left him craving for more.

At 18:30, on the night of the meal, Julius, Skye and Faith set off to meet Maks in New Satras. Morgana had told them that the matrix for their clothing had been embedded into the simulation programme, so they didn't need to worry about anything except turning up. This news had made them all very happy, as it took some of the pressure off.

'How're you feeling?' asked Julius, to Faith.

'As ready as I'll ever be,' he said, nervously.

'Be confident,' said Julius. 'You've worked hard for tonight.'

'That's right,' added Skye. 'Just be calm, relaxed and delicate. No sudden movements. And think before you speak. In fact, remember that you have two ears and one mouth; use them in that order.'

'Right,' nodded Faith, making mental notes. 'Listen first, talk later.'

'Correct,' continued Skye. 'Girls like an attentive listener. And don't forget the details; little things are important to them. Let her sit first, fill her glass if necessary, ask her questions that require more than just a yes or no answer, like I taught you.'

'What, who, why, which,' recited Faith, diligently.

'And after dinner, when we all go for a walk along the beach–'

'How do you know *that* will happen?' asked Faith, flustered.

'Why else do you think we're going to a romantic tropical island?' answered Skye. 'They want us to walk them along the shore in the moonlight. It's romantic. It gets them all fuzzy and dreamy.'

'You should write a book, man,' said Julius, enjoying the lesson.

'I kinda did, actually,' replied Skye. 'When List asked for my help with the sim-dating programme, I had to write a lot of this stuff down for the software.'

Julius chuckled. 'Please continue, master.'

'The moonlight walk is the right time to compliment her on a thing or two, like her dress, or her hair. Your mum's Italian, and Siena comes from Italy, so talk about that. Her reaction should tell you if she's ready.'

'For what?' asked Faith.

'You'll need to take her hand, no? Assuming she lets you, you can then move to arm-over-shoulder.'

'Like when?'

'I can't time you, now can I?'

'Oh, right, sure.'

'When you see a nice spot, lead her there and sit down. Talk some more and then ... then ...'

'Then *what*?'

'Well, then you're on your own.'

'Don't worry, Faith,' said Julius. 'You'll know what to do.'

'I hope so,' said Faith taking a deep breath.

When they got to the holographic sector, Maks was waiting by one of the entrances. They greeted him and walked to their holosuite, growing more curious by the minute. Skye entered the password Farrah had sent them and, when the door slid open, the four of them stepped inside.

Julius was once again reminded of how fantastic the holoworld was; as his sandal-clad feet sunk into the cool evening sand, there was nothing to remind him where he really was. His heavy-cottoned uniform had transformed into a loose, white linen outfit, comprising a shirt with rolled up sleeves, and trousers, which felt comfortable against his skin.

'Grand!' said Faith. 'Me legs are back!'

Julius grinned. It was a nice touch, and one that would certainly boost Faith's confidence. Looking around at the others, he noticed that they were all wearing similar, light coloured clothing and leather sandals. 'I'm sure they loved creating our clothes,' he said.

'And I bet you even our underwear is matching,' added Maks, peaking inside his trousers. 'White.'

The others confirmed the same, after a quick check.

'I wish *I* could have dressed *them*,' said Skye, dreamily.

'Knowing you, I'm not sure *they* would have liked that,' said Julius.

'Yeah, probably,' admitted Skye, as an afterthought.

Julius began to stroll away from the entrance, and was soon followed by the others. As he looked around, a sense of familiarity grew in him, as if somehow, he had been here before, though he had no clear memory of when, or even where exactly this was. The sun had already sunk beyond the horizon, leaving streaks of oranges and pinks in the evening sky. The sea was calm, and waves gently lapped against the shore, creating a serene melody all of their own.

'Over there,' said Faith, pointing towards a hut in the distance.

Julius looked, and saw that it was a circular structure, with a roof seemingly made of knitted palm leaves. An open-air kitchen stood to one side of it, and a bar on the other; at the front of the hut was a long patio, which held a wonderfully decorated table, set for eight people. Everything was illuminated by the flickering light of the many tall torches, planted in the sand, creating a soft atmosphere.

As they approached the small structure, a virtual waiter approached them, carrying a tray of colourful looking drinks. He was wearing a bright, flowery shirt, which matched the rest of the tropical appearance of the place. 'Good evening!' he greeted. 'Make yourselves at home.'

'Don't mind if I do,' said Skye, grabbing one the glasses.

Julius picked a cream coloured one, with a wedge of pineapple stuck to the rim. 'Cheers, guys,' he said, lifting his glass.

'Likewise,' replied Maks.

'Cheers,' said Faith and Skye.

Just then, the noise of girlish giggles carried to them from the other side of the bar.

'They're coming,' said Maks.

Julius detected a hint of excitement in his voice, and suddenly realised how excited he personally was, as well. Even after 82 days of going out with Farrah — not that he was counting or anything — the thought of seeing her, still made him feel as if it was for the first time. On cue, his palms began to sweat. He decided it might be wise to put his glass down before he could drop it, and wiped his hands on his trousers.

The girls emerged from behind the bar and Skye stepped forward promptly, heading for Valentina, arms opened. Julius opted to follow him, rather than wait for the girls to approach them. Using Skye as a sort of shield, he went straight over to Farrah. He was aware of Morgana as she walked past him, but he didn't look at her: first of all, he just wanted to see *his* girl.

Farrah was wearing a long, fuchsia, fitted dress, with thin shoulder straps. Her hair was softly gathered up, leaving only a few honey coloured curls loose to bounce against her slender neck. A pink lily was fixed one side of her head, matching a smaller one, which was pinned to a wrist strap.

As she stepped towards him, one long, tanned thigh slipped briefly into view, leaving Julius simply mystified. 'She comes with legs ...' he whispered, as a pleasant warm feeling rose in the pit of his stomach.

'And cleavage ...' breathed Faith, to his left, admiring Siena as if for the first time.

Farrah stopped in front of Julius, and they stared at each other for a few seconds.

'How do I look?' she asked, nervously.

'Drop dead gorgeous,' he said, proudly.

Farrah blushed, as one of her huge, dazzling smiles lit up her face. She stepped forward and kissed him gently. 'Come.'

Julius let her led him over to the table, where he greeted the other girls. Morgana was wearing a short, black summer dress; her long, dark hair was gathered in a ponytail. He couldn't help but notice how good she looked. He sat down on the same side of the table as her, but with Faith and Siena between them. Farrah took the chair opposite him, with Skye, Valentina and Maks seated to her right.

'This looks wonderful,' said Faith.

'Aye,' added Julius. 'A great idea.'

'Farrah did most of the thinking,' said Siena.

'I couldn't have done it without you, girls,' she replied quickly.

'Let's toast then,' said Skye, encouraging the others to take up their glasses. 'To our amazing ladies, who were able to concoct the perfect setting for our celebrations.'

'Hear, hear,' said Morgana cheerfully.

'A toast to the success of our missions,' continued Skye. 'To those that have been, and those that are still to come. And, last but not least, to Faith, for fulfilling one of his dreams. Well done, mate.'

'Thank you, guys,' said Faith, blushing.

'All right,' said Valentina, 'that's enough toasts for one night. Let's eat.'

'She's definitely with *you*,' said Julius to Skye.

'And for good reason,' he replied, flexing his biceps.

Farrah gestured to the waiter, who quickly summoned the help of several others. They brought a host of large, wooden trays, filled with grilled langoustines, king prawns, crabs and scallops, garnished with fresh herbs and wedges of large, juicy lemons.

Julius' mouth began to water at the sight. 'Bring it on,' he said, unfolding a napkin over his legs.

'Wow,' said Skye. 'Food that fights back. I like it.'

The first course was indeed a challenge, with the boys determined to get every last bit of meat from the shell-fishes, using all of the cutlery at their disposal. At one point, Skye even tried to pull out his Omni-gizmo to help him with the lobster, but Valentina held him back. 'Leave room for dessert, dear,' she told him.

The shellfish was followed by more, equally tasty dishes, like spicy plaice with mango, black olive and tomato salsa; pesto and olive-crusted monkfish, and plenty of salad to accompany everything.

As a tribute to her boyfriend, Farrah had even ordered a whale-sized, beer-battered, fish and chips, which left Julius gaping. 'Fish supper ...' he said, his Scottish accent resurfacing strongly.

'I never thought I would see one again,' said Morgana, similarly impressed. 'Well done, Farrah!'

'I thought you'd like it,' she said sweetly to him.

'What's this? What's this?' asked Skye, excited at the prospect of trying a new food.

'You're gonna love it, mate,' said Julius, dividing it into small portions and dishing them out to everyone.

'Here,' said Morgana, passing around a bowl that came with it. 'Put some tartare sauce on it.'

Julius excitedly explained how important it was to have a good "Chippy" on your street — something his dad had always raved about — with Morgana nodding approvingly. Faith was possibly the only other one who could properly appreciate Julius' little speech, while the rest of the group listened curiously.

'And you say some people put *vinegar* on it?' asked Maks.

'Or brown sauce,' added Morgana. 'At least in Edinburgh, we do.'

'Brown, you say?' said Skye, as if he was making mental notes.

'It's sort of vinegary too, but thick ... and brown,' she explained, before tucking into her fish with gusto.

After the last chip had disappeared from their plates, everyone agreed that it was time for dessert. The waiters promptly returned with small pastries, Italian style, in honour of Siena, along with coffee and tea.

'So, Africa's next,' said Maks, stirring his coffee. 'Anyone in your year from there?'

'Chiddy Dumisai is from Zimbabwe,' said Faith, passing the sugar to Siena.

'And there's Femi,' added Morgana, 'from Egypt. Mariam Richards is from Lebanon, but we don't know if her family will be there, or with the Asian folks.'

'It'll be a big one,' said Maks. 'I'd say roughly 40 days, if they manage to port an average of 20 million people per day.'

'That sounds about right,' agreed Julius. 'I still can't believe that the artefact was really a map.'

'Aye,' said Morgana. 'Well worth the detention we got for it.'

'Who's the Voice for Africa?' asked Farrah.

'Hasani Yeboah,' answered Skye. 'From Ghana.'

'I still think that finding the first location was kind of a miracle,' said Maks.

'Don't get me started on that one,' said Faith. 'I can't believe that we did that just by following the Taurus One's signature.'

'Yes, but since they won't tell us the truth, we'll just have to be content with that explanation,' said Valentina.

Julius was sure that Faith was right, but he had no way of proving it either.

As people finished their coffees, Julius heard Faith whispering to Siena, and asking if she would like to go for a walk. It must have taken all of his courage, and made Julius all the more proud of him; he was delighted to see Siena nodding enthusiastically in reply.

'Ladies,' said Faith, standing. 'I must thank you all once more for a splendid dinner.'

Skye winked at Julius, satisfied by this show of gallantry.

'Siena and I are going to admire the scenery,' he continued, helping her up.

'It was a pleasure, Faith,' replied Farrah. 'See you later!'

'I want to go too,' said Valentina dragging Skye from his chair.

'As you wish,' he said, grinning. 'Later, guys!'

At that point, Farrah and Morgana also stood, hinting that the others should follow suit.

Julius left his sandals behind and, when he was sure that the others had all gone ahead, he pulled Farrah to him, so that her body was pressed against his, and kissed her. 'It was a great dinner,' he said, afterwards. 'Thank you.'

'Glad you liked it.' She slipped her left hand into his right, and led him toward the shore.

The moon was full, bathing the sand and palm trees around them in milky light. Far ahead, Julius could see Faith and Siena walking side by side, while the others had gone off in the opposite direction. They walked in silence for a while, just enjoying the moment. Eager as he was to have her close to him whenever possible, he passed his arm around her shoulders, kissing her head as she drew near. It was then that he spotted the tall coconut tree from his dream, or at least one that looked just like it.

'What is it?' asked Farrah.

'That tree ... I've seen it before.'

'Let's go sit there, then,' she said.

Julius followed her, and the first thing he did was examine the base of its trunk. A look of disappointment crossed over his face. 'Hmm ... I was sure I was going to find a little carving there.'

'Something like "J+F"?' she said, grinning.

Julius looked at her, puzzled. 'As a matter of fact, yes. That's *exactly* what I was thinking. Are you reading my mind now?'

'I can read you like an open book, mister,' she said, teasingly.

Julius sat down on the sand, his back against the trunk. He let Farrah sit between his legs, resting with her back against him. 'Are you cold, Miss I-know-everything?'

In reply, she wrapped his arms around her, like a shawl. 'There, now it's better. I love to feel your arms around me. It makes me feel safe.'

Julius kissed her left cheek, breathing in her scent. 'You know,' he said, looking at her, 'it may sound odd but, every time I see you, there's something different about you.'

'What do you mean?'

'I'm not sure how to explain it, but you're not like the other 4th year girls.'

'Are you saying I look old?' she said, pretending to be offended.

'Never mind. I didn't mean it like that,' he said, poking her in the side.

'Well, what did you mean? Why am I not like the other girls?'

Julius thought that through, before answering. 'You're more mature, I think, like a *grown up*.'

'Maybe,' she said, giggling. 'And that is a nice thing to hear. Does that mean you're not bored of me yet?'

'How could I be?' he said, nuzzling her neck. 'You're ... addictive.' Each word was punctuated with a kiss.

'Hey, did I ever tell you about my secret hideout?'

'No,' answered Julius.

'It doesn't actually exist,' she explained. 'At least I don't think so. It's a place I've seen in my dreams, ever since I was really young.'

'Tell me about it,' said Julius, curious to find out more.

'It happens only when I'm in hospital. See, they need to put me into a sort of induced coma every time I go in,' she told him, candidly.

Julius nodded, although the news made him even more worried about her mysterious condition.

'I can't remember when the first time I dreamt about it was, but it felt good ... safe. After that, every time I was called back for check-ups, I knew that I could hide in Eneamar.'

'Eneamar? So you've even named it?'

Farrah shook her head. 'I think that's its *actual* name. I heard it spoken when I walked through the city streets, by the locals. Am I making sense?'

Julius laughed. 'No actually, but I'm having fun. Go on.'

'The city is beautiful, built on a sea of emerald green water. Clean air, clean streets, and blue skies. The sky-scrapers are bent in the shapes of arches, all made of glass. There are flower beds along the pavements, full of colourful plants and there is music in the air, a soft, soothing melody. It talks to you. "Everything will be alright," it says.'

Julius could tell by her voice, that she really liked this place and that it certainly had a strong effect on her. 'What about the people?'

'They aren't human,' she answered. 'They look a lot like us, but they are different. The most advanced beings in their galaxy. Their features are more delicate, their necks longer. Their skin is almost translucent and their eyes are always shining like crystals, no matter what colour they are. The women wear their hair in plaits, gathered to the back in the most beautiful hairstyles. I really wish it was real.' Farrah was silent for a while, as if her mind was still lost in this city. Then she turned around to look at Julius, a serious expression on her face. 'If I should ... go away, would you still remember me?'

'What?' said Julius, startled.

'Good things don't always last,' she said. There was a calm certainty in her voice, which scared him.

'What's going on? Is this because of your illness?'

Farrah smiled at him, but her eyes began to well up. To Julius, it looked as if she was struggling mentally with something. 'You know we can talk about anything, right?' he told her, gently.

'You're the best thing that has ever happened to me,' she said, 'and I'm really, really scared of losing you.'

'You won't,' he answered, holding her by the shoulders. 'I'll be by your side till the end.'

She lunged forward and kissed him. Julius held her tight, kissing her back, a mixture of feelings taking hold of him. Why had she said that? Had the doctor recalled her to the hospital? He needed to find out, but maybe now wasn't the right time. As he lay on the sand with her, wiping the tears from her face with his lips, he knew it wasn't. Tonight was for them.

CHAPTER 10

INTO THE NIGHT

The African mission hit the ground running. The Mizkis' lessons had once again been suspended, and the students prepped in advance so that, when the small red planet finally came into view, they were all ready to go. A fleet of Zed officers had been sent ahead to scout the airspace above the underground compound where they had registered the presence of the bio-signatures, and its landing area. They returned, confirming what everyone had already been expecting: the resistance found was nothing more than a show. A brief and vicious struggle had taken place between a dozen Arneshian planes and the Cougars, which had ended with the enemy being completely wiped out. With the coast clear, the huge portals were fitted around Moonrising, as they had done during the Oceania rescue and, just like then, Julius and his classmates boarded the Cougars, to provide aerial support.

The mood was light and cheery that morning, and the sense of satisfaction was tangible among the students: it was the first day of the rescue mission, but victory was already in the air.

'Goshawk, ready to go,' confirmed Julius to the tower, before lifting off. He could see Faith up ahead of him, leaving the hangar with a brio he hadn't shown in months, and that was all thanks to Siena. Julius chuckled as he recalled how his friend had come knocking at his door the morning after the meal, to share some good news, and thank Skye for the extra lessons. Apparently, he must have made quite an impression, since Siena hadn't just kissed him back, but had also immediately agreed to go steady with him. So now, Faith was all loved-up, grinning like a loon and using phrases like 'me wild nymph', whenever he mentioned her.

Speaking of being loved-up, Julius knew he really needed to be careful himself because, the more time he spent with Farrah, the more he felt utterly under her spell. Just thinking about that Saturday night left him feeling all flustered, as images of his hand running along her toned, soft thigh kept repeating on a loop in his head. One of his favourite highlights was when he had slid his hand up the back of her leg and up toward her–

'Watch it, McCoy!' cried Morgana, through their toon channel com-link.

Julius veered just in time to avoid bumping into the side of her Cougar. 'Sorry!' he said, panicking. 'Are you all right?'

'Yeah,' she said, sounding a little miffed. 'Just watch where you're going.'

'I know what he's watching,' said Skye with a chuckle. 'And I'm sure it wasn't the portal!'

'Very funny,' said Julius, drily.

'In fact, I've been meaning to ask you, it *was* you who triggered the safe-relationship protocol on Saturday night, right?'

'Look who's talking!' joined in Faith.

'Yeah!' added Julius, 'As far as I know, it could have been *you*, Miller.'

'Hey, I wrote that programme, remember? That's why we left early!'

'Why, you sneaky son-of-a-gun. You could have told us!'

Skye was laughing his head off at that point. 'Anyway,' he said, once he had composed himself, 'I bet it was Morgana. It's always the quiet ones.'

'Just you wait till we get out of these planes, Skye Miller,' said Morgana, only half-seriously, 'and I'll show you *quiet*.'

'Oh yeah, baby. I'll be waiting,' he added in a husky voice that made her giggle.

'OK, that's enough! Let's focus, people,' cut in Julius quickly. 'We have a mission at hand.' There was still simply no way he could be part of a conversation which required him to imagine Morgana doing anything that would trigger the safe-relationship protocol. Actually, now that he thought about it, it might even have been him who had set it off, possibly when Farrah had removed– No that was *not* good. He shook his head clear of such thoughts, and put aside all memories of the party. Much safer that way.

Over the next three weeks, all the Mizkis had their days divided up into three, eight-hour shifts, filled with aerial support, rest and data entry. The absence of any Arneshian counterattack made Julius quite nervous. He kept asking himself why. Where were the Nuarns, and why had T'Rogon moved them to Arnesh — if that's where they really were. Julius tried hard to guess what Freja would do next. On the one hand, there were two more continents to rescue, which were quite a fair distance away from each other; on the other hand, the Taurus constellation, home of Salgoria, was relatively close to their current position — a matter of a few small hyperjumps, in fact.

'I wish adults were more open with us,' he said to himself one night as he was returning, inside his Cougar, to

Tijara's hangar. It wasn't only the mission he was thinking about; he was, of course, thinking about his classified file and whatever plans Freja had in store for him. 'And when is all that supposed to happen, anyway?' he wondered. Julius knew that he had had little enough time to see Farrah properly, but they were now halfway through the rescue, and his birthday was only a few days away. Surely they would give him a break for that.

On Thursday the 18th of April, Julius received a most welcome present. The Skirts had decided to pull a few double shifts, in order to get him the whole day off. Once Clavel had given his permission for this, they met with him at breakfast and told him the news.

'You guys are the best!' he said, hugging them each in turn. 'Thank you!'

'Oh, it's all right,' said Faith. 'But don't forget to meet us tonight for dinner.'

'I won't,' said Julius. 'Where are we going, by the way?'

'Not sure yet,' said Morgana. 'New place, perhaps. We'll text you later.'

Julius left them with a spring in his step, destination New Satras. He thought he would surprise Farrah by telling her that they had time for more than just dinner together. She had already arranged to get the evening off from duties, by working the afternoon shift. Because of that, he hoped she would be free this morning too. As he headed to her parents' shop, he was as excited as a kid in a candy store.

When Julius entered Auld Oddities, the door swung inwards, and a little bell tinkled. This unfamiliar feature took him aback, as all of the doors in his life were of the automatic, sliding variety. 'It must be part of the shop's presentation,' he thought, amused.

The front room was empty, but he could hear a female voice talking in the back of the shop, possibly Farrah's mother. It sounded like she was on a call, so Julius decided to wait and peruse the shelves, which were laden with all manner of curious and bizarre items. He felt a little awkward being there; after all, he had never been properly introduced to Farrah's parents. What if she hadn't mentioned him to them? What if they didn't even know that she had a boyfriend? Maybe he should pretend that he was just a schoolmate, to avoid causing any trouble for Farrah. Agreeing with himself that this was the sensible thing to do, he resumed his rounds. He was just examining a curious item, labelled "record player", when his eyes caught sight of something unexpected. A picture had been placed above the counter, in a beautiful gold, wooden frame. The scene portrayed a young couple holding a little blonde girl, of no more than six or seven years old, who was wearing a red-and-white dress, with shiny black shoes and short, white socks. Surrounding the happy family were none other than the three GMs of Zed: Freja, Milson and Kloister. What really caused Julius to do a double-take on it, however, was that he knew exactly when and where that picture had been taken; it had been on the 1st of December of the previous year, in Satras, the day of the deadline for Faith's spaceship competition. Julius clearly remembered how, after visiting Pete's shop, they had all gone to eat at Hallouminati and that, while they had been sitting there, he had noticed the little girl lifting huge objects with a mere flick of her wrist. The mother had called her by name that day - what was it again? Indeed, the woman holding the girl in the picture was Mrs Hendricks, and Julius assumed the man to be her husband. He wondered if the girl was Farrah's cousin, or something, because he could definitely see a resemblance there, and she had certainly never mentioned having a sister.

'Can I help you?'

Julius whirled around, startled. 'Uh, good morning, ma'am. I'm a friend of Farrah. Is she here?'

The woman looked at him with what seemed like just a hint of diffidence. 'What is your name?'

'Julius, ma'am; Julius McCoy,' he said, bowing slightly.

'Oh,' she said, instantly becoming tenser. 'Farrah is at the hospital.'

'The hospital? Is she all right?'

'It's just a regular checkup.'

'Is there something I can do for her?' he said quickly, unable to ignore the fact that she wasn't really forthcoming with her answers.

Mrs Hendricks paused at that question, as if some internal dilemma was taking place in her mind. Eventually, she shook her head and smiled. 'Thank you, Julius, but there's nothing you can do right now. She'll be back later on in the afternoon.'

Those words reassured him a little; she was fine and he would be able to see her as planned. In the meantime, though, he wasn't sure how to spend the rest of the morning, so he headed toward the lifts, where he knew there was a large interactive map of New Satras. The games were down while the mission was ongoing, so he hoped to get some inspiration on what to do, from exploring the directory.

As the escalator took him up to his destination, Julius noticed a door, set within a recess, and his mind took a quick leap back in time. He recalled now that it was in fact the same door he had waited in front of, while a wave of Mizkis passed him by, on the day when he had first met Farrah. He remembered the strange heat that had emanated from it, so hot that it had almost burned his neck, and the strange symbol etched into its surface, of 4 interlinked stars, forming a diamond shape. Suddenly, Julius' eyes grew wide, as he remembered exactly where else he had seen that symbol, not once, but twice before. He took the remaining escalator steps two at the time, and boarded the lift for Tijara, everything else instantly forgotten.

Ten minutes later, Julius was in the training sector, staring at a closed door. He had returned to the little storage room where Foster had sent him and Faith for their detention. The corridor was empty, so no-one was about to question what he was doing there; quickly, he opened the door and stepped into the room. Using his PIP to light the way, he found the light switch and flicked it on. The shelves were filled with the items that he and Faith had unpacked that night, seemingly untouched and unused since then.

'Where are you?' he muttered, as he searched the shelves. He quickly worked his way from the top shelf towards the bottom one. 'Bingo,' he said out loud, a few minutes later. It was still there after all. "Tijara's Ultimate Sacrifice", he read, as he pulled it out, looking at the cover of the microchip: it had four stars joined by straight lines, in the shape of a diamond on it, the exact same emblem that was on the cover of his classified file. Julius searched the room for a chip reader, and found one lying on top of a stack of boxes. It was a circular device, not larger than his own hand; he placed it on the floor, and sat in front of it. Delicately, he inserted the chip into the empty slot and waited.

A hologram of Marcus Tijara sprang suddenly to life above the pad. It wasn't actual size, so Julius was able to look him straight in the eyes. Marcus looked just like he did in his many portraits: short dark hair, tall and sturdy, with a curious glint in his light brown eyes. It was a likeable face, welcoming and friendly. To each side of Tijara, there were various text headings, which Julius began to scan quickly. One entry simply read "Tijara's Heart", a title Julius instantly recognised from his file. He touched his right index finger to the heading and leaned back against the wall, holding his breath.

'The device is now completed,' said Marcus, a strange mix of sadness and satisfaction etched across his features.

Julius liked his voice immediately: it was deep and caring; somehow perfectly fitting with the image of Marcus he had built up in his head.

'I didn't think it was possible, but there it is: Tijara's Heart. This is my last gift to Zed; its last defence. They asked me why I've called it so. I have used my own name for it, because only I can use it, a White Child. As for the Heart, well, let's just say that a lot will be given up for the sake of humanity. That, and the fact that this device is for the undying love of my life, to whom my heart had already been given a long time ago. Maybe afterwards, we shall once again be able to live as a family, in peace. For her, this is a sacrifice I am willing to make. I only wish I had more time to test the crys–'

The recording crackled and stopped abruptly. Frustrated, Julius switched the reader off. He knew that Marcus was referring to Clodagh Arnesh, when he spoke of his undying love. The rest of the message however, was a little too cryptic to understand. Tijara's Heart was to be used for the defence of Zed, that much was clear; it involved some sort of sacrifice on the part of the giver and, by all accounts, it looked like he was next in line. He needed to know more, so he opened his PIP, and called the only person he thought would be able to help him. 'Mr Hastings?'

'Julius?' replied the Curiate. 'Are you OK?'

'I am, sir. Sorry to disturb you at work, but ... I need to ask you ... what do you know about Tijara's Heart.'

Ben seemed to consider his answer for a moment. 'Let's meet.'

Julius went back to the holo-floor of New Satras, where Ben was waiting for him by the large screens. As he joined the Curiate and they found a seat in the courtyard, a feeling of dread spread over him.

'What do you know of Tijara's death?' asked Ben, eventually.

'Only that he died in the final battle with Clodagh,' answered Julius.

'Technically yes, he did, but it was by his own hand.'

'How so?'

'The Heart was a machine he had built for that last stand and, as he used it against the Arneshians, he also gave himself up. *He* was the sacrifice. There was no other way to power the weapon, except with his own life energy. But, why are you asking about this?'

Julius had turned white. It took him a while before he could speak again. 'I found a chip in a storage room, called "Tijara's Ultimate Sacrifice". It had a symbol on it, the same one that was on my classified file. You were right: Freja has marked me down for one final mission. He wants me to activate Tijara's Heart again.'

'How do you know that?' asked Ben, looking perplexed.

'I broke into his office, and saw the file,' replied Julius.

Hastings seemed at a loss for words.

'Don't feel bad,' said Julius. 'I knew you weren't supposed to tell me, but now I need to know everything.'

'I'm sorry all the same, Julius,' said Ben. He stood up and took a few steps into the arena, before turning back to him. 'What do you want to know?'

'If Tijara's Heart was the *ultimate* weapon, why are we having this conversation? Why weren't the Arneshians killed off once and for all?'

'Because that was not the purpose of the device,' answered Ben. 'Marcus wasn't a mass murderer; he just wanted the Arneshians out of the game. The Heart does not remove life, but power. You need to understand how the Arneshians work, Julius. All of them have what we call a "Pearl" of White skills inside them, which activate their Grey skills.'

'Is that why my brother could levitate socks?'

'Yes. It's also why some people can be misread during the induction test.'

Julius thought of Billy Somers, a proper case of *misreading*, if ever there was one.

'The Heart was invented to block these Pearls,' continued Ben, 'which in turn would deactivate their Grey skills, transforming the Arneshian carrier into a simple, albeit slightly more logical, human, but nothing more.'

'What happens to Nuarns and people like us?'

'There were *no* Nuarns back then, so I don't know. As for us, our Pearls are far too big to be damaged by the weapon. Anyway, when Clodagh arrived with the largest fleet humanity had ever seen, Marcus was ready. The machine delivered in full and the *new* Arneshians had to kneel before its superiority. The war ended in that instant. They retreated with their tails between their legs, all except for Clodagh.'

'How did she die?'

'Before the device went off, she went looking for Marcus where the Heart was kept. People saw her shuttle docking beside his and, after a while, there was an explosion. And that, as they say, was that.'

'I have to ask again,' said Julius. 'Why are we having this conversation if Marcus was successful?'

'Many reasons,' replied Ben, sitting back next to him. 'Not all the Arneshians were in the fleet. The ones left behind bided their time, repopulated their planet, regrouped, all those things. Also, Marcus wasn't as strong as you are now, nor did he have your augmented powers. The Curia really believes that this time would be the last, if we attack their home-world directly.'

'Am I supposed to ... die too?' asked Julius, eventually.

'*What?* Of course not,' said Ben, putting his hand on Julius' shoulder. 'I told you that Freja is reckless when it comes to the school, but he's no murderer.'

'So ... what am I supposed to sacrifice, then?'

Ben looked at him. 'Your powers, Julius. All of them.'

The words landed like a stone hitting the bottom of a well, leaving Julius breathless and stupefied. He tried to say something, but his mouth had gone dry and his lips wouldn't part. He watched as Ben sat quietly by his side, waiting. 'You might as well kill me,' he managed, eventually.

Ben chuckled humourlessly. 'Yeah, I'm with you on that, as you well know.'

'So that's it,' said Julius. 'Freja has set me apart for this one-way trip, without even asking me.'

'I suppose he should have,' said Ben. 'Or at least one of us was supposed to break it to you. When you called me before, I let him know that I would be the one to do it. I hope you don't mind — believe me, he was relieved that someone else took the job. Technically you're the only one that can man that machine, Julius; and your life belongs to Zed, after all. You didn't sign up for your own glory, you know?'

'This feels like "humanity's last hope" type of crap,' said Julius, who was too furious to worry about watching his words anymore. 'Why now? Why can't I try some other way? Why do I have to sacrifice all I have, all I *am*? Why?' In his mind, those words were really translating as, '*Why, now that I have Farrah?*'

'Look, you're a good kid; if you really wanted to, I could give you a way out. I could guarantee safe passage to somewhere on the regular colonies where no one knows who you are. You'd be in hiding yes, but with your mind-skills intact. But, do you really want that?'

Julius didn't answer. He took a breath and asked, 'When is this supposed to happen?'

'1st of May,' replied Ben. 'On that day, we'll be at the closest co-ordinates to the Taurus constellation, where Arnesh is. You have 12 days to inform Freja of your decision.'

'Huh,' grunted Julius, running his fingers through his hair. 'I really don't think I want to talk to him, actually.'

'Call me, then. If it's of any consolation, your girlfriend wasn't going to be sticking around either.'

Julius looked up quickly. 'What do you mean?'

'Since you've already read your file, you know that you weren't supposed to meet FH,' he said knowingly.

'She *is* the one from my file, then. Why not?'

'She's not who you think she is, Julius. I feel bad telling you this, but given the kind of decision you're about to make, I think it's fair someone levels with you. It may even help you.'

'Go on,' he said. His voice had gone cold.

'She's 15, going on 21. Every one of your years, is roughly seven of hers. She's the Oracle's treasure, the one you rescued from Angra Mainyu; the daughter of Marcus and Clodagh.'

'That's impossible!' he cried, leaping up. 'It was destroyed. The GMs said so. You're just making this up.'

Ben shook his head. 'She wasn't supposed to try the Solo game, but she did anyway. Of course, she beat you and everyone else on that scoreboard, being who she is, but that's why her game and score haven't been broadcasted. They are classified. If you think your powers are strong, you haven't seen anything yet. Compare to her you're a newbie.'

'But ... her parents?'

'They're undercover Zed officers. They took her in as an infant, a couple of years ago. Even without this chat we're having, she would have had to disappear, in the near future. That's why she joined Sield this year; she wasn't old enough before then. Think of it like this, Julius: by the time you're 20, she'll be close to her fifties.'

Julius slumped back down, feeling utterly bewildered. The picture in Auld Oddities had been of Farrah. He had seen her with his own two eyes, only a year ago. No wonder she seemed different to him every time they met — she was ageing. It would also explain why her mother didn't look anything like her. And what about the tropical setting of their dinner? All those details, from the palm tree to the white sand. "I can read you like an open book" she had told him on the beach. It looks like she wasn't kidding. 'How do I know you're not lying to me?' said Julius, grasping at one last glimmer of hope.

'Ask her yourself,' he said, standing up. 'You have a big decision ahead of you.'

'You said I have no choice.'

'We *always* have a choice. This is yours and yours alone. I wish I could help you more, but ... Happy birthday, for what it's worth, Julius.'

Julius didn't stand to say goodbye, nor did he watch Ben as he walked away. He just sat there, for what felt like an eternity.

'Julius!' cried Farrah, before running across Rowan Square to meet him.

Julius didn't move, nor did he uncross his arms. He just stood there, by the tree where he had first met her.

Farrah must have felt that something was wrong because, as she drew nearer, her run had turned to a walk. 'What's happened?'

Against every bit of his will, which made him want to hold her tight, he steeled himself away from her. 'Why did you lie to me?'

The words, spoken quietly, had the effect of cold water on Farrah, who stopped dead in her tracks, the smile disappearing from her face. 'I didn't know what else to do,' she said simply, and slumped down on the bench facing the tree.

'You didn't, huh?' said Julius, bitterly. 'How about NOT letting me into your life in the first place, knowing that you were going to leave me sooner or later? How did you put it, the other night, on the beach? "Good things don't always last." Smooth, Farrah. Very smooth.'

'Do you think I chose this?' she retorted, starting to lose her cool. She stood and walked up to him. 'Did I *choose* to be abandoned by my own mother even before I was born? Did I *choose* to be found by you, or to be handed over to a couple of soldiers for parents? I did not! And, most definitely, I did *not* choose to fall in love with you!'

'This isn't love,' replied Julius, his voice raising. 'Love means sacrifice, but you've been selfish.'

'How?' she asked, her eyes widening in surprise.

'You *knew* this couldn't last and you let it happen anyway. You should have let me go,' he said, not caring that he probably sounded unfair or illogical just then.

Farrah it seems, couldn't find a reply to that. Tears began to well in her eyes, but she didn't wipe them away. 'You said you'd be by my side till the end ...'

'This *is* the end,' replied Julius. He turned and walked away, without looking back.

Julius didn't show up for his birthday meal. He simply texted Skye to say that he had broken up with Farrah. It worked perfectly, because no one asked him any questions about his skulking mood. The Skirts must have warned a few of the other Mizkis too, who did their best to stay away from him with any probing questions.

To the eyes of all, Julius was dealing with a harsh case of a broken heart, but inside, in spirit, he was in agony. Every time he had to use his powers, which was quite a lot since he was piloting the Cougars for the rescue mission, he couldn't help but think about how it would soon be his last time using them. Whenever he crossed one of his teachers in the corridors of Moonrising, he remembered all that he had accomplished over the past four years of training. It was the exceptional things he could do that made it particularly hard to decide; like the inorganic draws he could perform, or the cascade of colourful wisps he was able to see, that made his view of the world so special.

To say that he was miserable was an understatement. Freja had asked him to let go of all the things in his life that made him who he was; but how could he let go of all his friends, or his future career as fleet captain? Even Michael would be more powerful than he was, if he went through with this.

The absence of Farrah from his life was crushing. It felt as if a part of his being had been removed and left empty. Sometimes, it was even physically painful. With the passing hours, he had distributed the blame equally between all of the GMs, on account of how they had lied the previous year when they had said the embryo would be destroyed; Farrah should have been better guarded and not allowed to interact with anybody. How they could possibly think it was good idea for her to join Sield, was beyond Julius to comprehend. After all, Freja practically knew how many times Julius went to the toilet, so he must have known that they were seeing each other. If they weren't meant to meet, then why had Freja allowed it to happen? On a logical level, Julius could see that they had let her live, for a while anyway, like a normal girl. It would be her only chance at that, but it was a broken-hearted young man who had to deal with the pain and there was no logic to set that particular wrong right. Frustrated by all of these thoughts, Julius would spend his evenings pacing up and down the corridors, avoiding making eye contact with anybody. He could see that Morgana was itching to talk to him, but he kept her at a distance and she didn't push him.

Ben had told him that he had a choice, even offering him an escape route. But the more he thought about it, the more he knew there was no easy way out. There was no honour in avoiding his responsibilities, and that is what it came down to in the end. He clearly remembered the talks he had had with Faith and Morgana. Their words had been haunting Julius in all the waking hours of these past few days. Faith had spoken about inner strength and how choosing his cousin's life over his own freedom to walk could never be questioned. "We all have responsibilities. She was mine," he had told Julius. His friend hadn't faltered then and, given the choice, Julius knew he would do it all over again. As for Morgana, she had clearly told him that he had been born a White Child for a reason — who was he to waste that gift? Even Ben had said that such a gift should be used to bring hope back to the people. And as far as his own fear was concerned, Julius now knew now what it was: to be normal and powerless.

The final push towards making a decision came on Tuesday night. Part of Julius really could not believe that Freja would send him on such a mission, without as much as a single word. Determined to hear it from the GM's own mouth, he walked towards his office to confront him. As he approached the corridor, he heard Cress and Freja talking behind the corner, so he stopped.

'We need to get McCoy ready,' said Freja.

'What if he says no?' asked Cress.

'It isn't his choice, Nathan.'

Julius was startled by the curtness of Freja's tone. Was there even a point in talking to him if he had no alternatives? Hurt, he turned on his heels and walked back to the dorms, a sense of betrayal growing in his heart.

When dawn broke on Wednesday the 1st of May, Julius was sitting cross-legged on the floor of his room, staring into space. A single tear had dried on his cheek, marking the end of his inner struggle. His mind was made up: he was no hero, but he was a very necessary link in an important chain. He had been dealt a special hand, and he was going to play it well. When Skye left the room, he called Hastings. 'I'm ready.'

'Do you want me to accompany you, or shall I call the GM?' asked Ben.

'I'd rather not see him,' said Julius. A brief thought went to Captain Kelly, but he felt it was too late to ask for that. Who knew where he was, anyway? 'Do *you* mind coming with me?'

'I'd be honoured,' he replied. 'Meet me in thirty minutes by the door in New Satras. You know the one I mean, right?'

Julius nodded. 'Till then,' he finished, before closing his PIP.

He went for a shower, and toyed with the idea of leaving a note for the others. He had decided not to tell them directly, in case they tried to stop him and, in truth, he was afraid that his resolve would falter if they pressed him hard enough. He dressed, took a good look around the room, not knowing if he would be allowed back once his powers had gone, and made his way to New Satras.

His heart was heavy, and he could hardly breathe properly. As he waited for the lift, he suddenly decided to send a short message. He selected the Skirts' group mail address and typed, "I've accepted Freja's mission. I'm going to use Tijara's Heart on Arnesh. Ben Hastings is taking me. I'll see you guys later." It was done; he would send it on his way to the Heart. There was nothing left to do now, except fulfill his duty.

CHAPTER 11

JULIUS' HEART

'Morning, folks,' said Skye, sitting down with his breakfast tray.

'Hi there,' replied Morgana, stifling a yawn.

'Where's WC?' asked Faith, stretching to look behind Skye, to see if he was following.

'I left him in the room. I think he was meditating.'

'Who? Julius?' said Morgana. 'Yeah, right.'

'Well, either that or he'd fallen asleep cross-legged, staring out the window.'

'Did we actually figure out what happened between him and Farrah?' asked Faith, poking at his cereal.

'Not me,' answered Skye. 'He's been very private about this whole business. He looks thoroughly miserable, though. What about you, Morgana?'

'No. In fact, no one has even seen Farrah at Sield since Julius' birthday, or so Maks told me. I wonder ...'

'Hmm?' said Skye, his mouth full.

'Just wondering if a split-up is all this is, actually. Julius has been so strange lately, like he's had something on his mind.' She shook her head. 'You know what he's like; he'd rather keep things to himself than ask for help.'

'Yeah, I know,' said Skye. 'Maybe it's time we corner him. What do you think?'

Faith looked at his PIP. 'We have some time before reporting for duty. We should go fetch him.' At that moment, his screen beeped. 'Wait, Skirts mail,' he said.

The others opened theirs too and read the message, as a mixture of shock and surprise took hold of them.

'I *knew* there was something else,' said Morgana, who was now extremely upset. 'Why didn't he talk to us?'

'Is he referring to the mission from the classified file?' asked Faith.

'It has to be,' answered Skye. 'Look at the name, "Tijara's Heart"; it's the same one that was on his file. And who's this Ben?'

'He's one of the Curiate,' said Morgana. 'You probably know them all.'

'Yes, I *do* know the Curiates, but none of them are called Ben,' said Skye, suddenly worried.

'What?' she said, stunned.

'Let's go find Freja,' said Faith, standing up and hurrying them out of the mess hall.

They ran across Moonrising at full pelt, past the dorms and the engine room, raising a few eyebrows as they went, until they reached the teacher's floor. As they turned one of the corners, they collided head-on with Freja and Master Cress.

'Watch where you're going, Mizkis,' said Cress, steadying Skye from falling.

'Sorry, sir,' said Faith, bowing quickly.

Something in their faces put Freja on alert. 'What's going on?'

'It's Julius, Grand Master,' said Morgana, panting. 'He's gone.'

Freja's astonishment instantly spread over his face. 'Explain yourself.'

In reply, Morgana opened her PIP and showed him the message.

Freja's eyes grew wide. 'When did you receive this message?'

'About 5 minutes ago,' answered Skye. 'What's happening?'

'Cress, get Kelly to track the Heart's signature and follow it. Prepare a fleet for Arnesh. Go!'

'Right away,' said Cress, sprinting towards the hangar.

'You three, come with me!' The urgency in his voice made the others realise just how serious the situation was.

'Grand Master,' asked Morgana, as she ran beside him. 'Is it true that Hastings isn't a Curiate? That he's not one of us?'

'There's no one by that name among the Curiates, Miss Ruthier,' replied Freja, coldly. 'But he's one of us all right. Or so we thought.'

Morgana looked at the others, her panic rising.

Freja entered one of the control rooms and walked straight to a monitor. The technician working there moved out of the way without uttering a word. The surveillance camera was pointed dead centre at the door by the lifts, in New Satras. Freja first checked the time, then placed his finger on the corner of the screen, moving it anti-clockwise, to rewind the recording.

The Skirts had gathered behind him, focusing intently on the screen, for a sign of anything unusual. A few seconds later, they found what they were looking for. Freja stopped, and turned the sound up. A heavy silence had fallen on the room. Julius came into view a few seconds later, and stopped by the door. He seemed extremely serious, with a deep line creasing his brow. Then he looked up, and stretched his right arm forward. A man came into view and shook his hand, before patting him on the shoulder in a reassuring manner.

'You're very brave, Julius,' said Ben, his voice loud in the stillness of the surveillance room. 'Braver than I could ever be. Zed will not forget what you're about to do.'

Julius nodded. 'Let's go, before I change my mind.'

Hastings pulled out some sort of key from his pocket — the sight of it seemed to stun Freja greatly — and placed it against the door. Immediately, the diamond emblem glowed into life, and the door unlocked.

'Welcome to Tijara's Heart,' said Ben.

Julius looked beyond the door, hesitating. Then he took a deep breath and stepped inside.

Ben followed him and the door swished shut behind him, leaving the camera staring at the symbol in its center.

Freja passed his hands over his face, looking momentarily lost. He seemed to have aged considerably in these last few minutes. He moved to the next monitor, which showed a view of space. Steadily, he rewound the recording, until the clock marked the time just after Julius had entered through the door. On the monitor, a ship flew out of Moonrising. It was a smaller craft, of a kind that hadn't been seen since the time of Marcus Tijara, flat as a disk and bronze in colour. A ring of lights, which revolved slowly around its circular hull, surrounded it. Steadily, it made its way away from Moonrising's orbit, then slipped into warp and disappeared from view.

'Sir,' said Skye, taking advantage of the silence. 'Even if Ben lied about his job, you were going to send Julius on that mission anyway. So why the bad feeling?'

Freja ignore the question, and asked one of his own in return. 'How did McCoy find out about Tijara's Heart?'

'Accidentally,' answered Morgana, quickly, avoiding any mention of Julius and Faith breaking into Cress' office. 'Ben Hastings confirmed it afterwards. Julius told me so himself.'

'Do you know what will happen to him if he uses the weapon?' asked Freja, seemingly dismissing Morgana's feeble explanation. He appeared to be calm, but his eyes told another story.

They shook their heads, their worries now surfacing fast.

'Assuming that Hastings really intends for McCoy to activate the Heart and use it against Arnesh, he will sacrifice every last strand of mind-skills he has. Forever. Without mentioning that he could very well die.'

'What?' cried Skye.

Faith looked horrified. 'But you ... you were going to send him there too!'

'Yes, I was,' said Freja, now visibly angry, 'but not without this!' he lifted a long, white crystal from his pocket and held it in front of them. 'Marcus Tijara himself designed it to preserve his own powers when he used the Heart, so that he could get them back afterwards.'

'Then we need to stop them!' implored Morgana.

'We will try, but it may be too late.'

'Don't say that, please,' she begged, tears beginning to flow down her cheeks. 'There must be something we can do. I don't care about his powers; I want *him* back!'

'Damn you, McCoy,' shouted Freja, slamming his fist on the console. 'Of all the stubborn Mizkis that ever passed through this school, why did it have to be *you*?' He turned to face the Skirts. 'How many times did I tell you not to go off on one, before talking to me? How many? Do you think I would have let him go on a trip like this without talking to him myself, or taking precautions? Huh? But no, you always know best. With this stunt he's jeopardising an entire mission, all that we've been working for in the last few years, not to mention his own powers. If that happens he will have brought it upon himself, and if you knew that he was going to go on this mission alone, then you are just as guilty as he is!'

The Skirts stood there in complete silence. Seeing Freja so upset was a unique and shocking experience. But the

Grand Master was right, and there was nothing they could say back to him.

'Sir,' said Cress, entering the room. 'Kelly was able to track their signatures and he's now in pursuit.'

'Send the coordinates to our fleet. He'll need back-up when he enters into Arnesh's airspace.'

'There's something else too,' continued Cress, looking at the Skirts, as if he was unsure if he should say it in front of them.

Freja decided for him. 'Well?'

'Miss Hendricks is also missing.'

The Grand Master looked stunned. He turned to the Mizkis, gravely. 'Go back to your duties. That's an order.'

Morgana was about to say something, but Skye pushed her gently out of the room before she could. 'If anyone can find them,' he whispered to her, 'Kelly will.'

The last thing they heard, before they left the room, was Freja demanding to know how they could have allowed this to happen.

Captain Kelly was in the ready room of the Ahura Mazda, sitting at the head of the table. Elian was to his left, with Master Cress on his right. Even now, Kelly felt the need to be physically separating them. His crew was still in pursuit of the Heart, along with a large Zed fleet, which had also joined them. The Tijara portion of Moonrising had also split from the rest of the battlestar, and Professor Beloi was trying to contact Julius telepathically as they moved in closer, in the slim hope of stopping him before it was too late.

'Nathan,' said Elian, 'how did this happen? Why did Julius go with the Arneshian without speaking to you or Carlos, first?'

'For starters, we didn't know McCoy had found out about the mission, let alone that we had a traitor in the Curia itself.'

'What do you mean?' asked Elian, looking shocked.

'Ben Hastings isn't an Arneshian; he's one of ours, a Zed officer working in the Curia.'

'What?'

'We don't know exactly when he switched sides, but last year must have been his big chance to impress Ambassador T'Rogon, and he obviously succeeded.'

'But how did Julius find out about this dratted mission?' said Kelly, feeling thoroughly frustrated.

'He broke into my office, if you really want to know,' answered Cress, with a raised eyebrow. 'He saw a classified file with his name on it by chance, when he came to see me, and snuck back in to read it. I cornered Shanigan earlier and, eventually, he admitted it. McCoy went with Hastings to use the weapon willingly; he may be a fool, but he has honour. He must have truly believed that he was doing the right thing. This Ben has been very clever: using the truth about the Heart and what it does, he led McCoy to do what Tijara himself had done before, appealing to his sense of duty. The only lie he told was in convincing Julius that we were working together.'

'If only you had been more open with him from the start,' said Kelly, coldly, 'all this would never have happened.'

'We made a mistake,' replied Cress.

'A mistake that could cost Julius his life. You're just like my father, Nathan: the school comes first. No wonder you get along so well.'

'What's *that* supposed to mean?' asked Nathan, angrily sitting up in his chair.

'Enough!' shouted Elian. 'The pair of you! What's done is done, so let's focus on the next bit, shall we?'

'Humph,' said Cress, but he did as Elian had asked.

Kelly also curbed his temper, he certainly didn't need an upset wife on top of all this. 'We'll be entering Arnesh's orbit very soon. Any idea what we're likely to find there?'

'Plenty of hostility, no doubt,' answered Cress. 'Only a handful of their fleet was deployed to guard the three compounds holding our people, which leads us to believe that the rest of them are still there, back on their home world. We're heading for serious fire.'

Kelly nodded. For a brief moment, he even considered asking Nathan to order Elian back to Moonrising, just in case things went bad, but he knew there was more chance of Salgoria surrendering than of Elian stepping away from the action. 'We'll be ready,' he said, silently hoping that they actually would be.

On and off, for the last ten minutes, Julius had begun to feel pretty uncomfortable. He had the definite feeling that something wasn't right. For starters, he could hear a strange sort of distant echo in the deep recesses of his mind but, no matter how hard he tried, he couldn't figure out what it was, or where it was coming from. It reminded him of a telepathic link under construction, yet, out here in the deep emptiness of space, who could possibly be trying to contact him? Then, there was the matter of *the smell.* It was too faint to clearly tell what it was, but it had distinctive traces of sweetness to it. Again, Julius struggled to identify it, knowing that it was somehow familiar to him. The truth was, that the closer they drew to Arnesh, the more it dawned on him that his destiny was coming to meet him with open arms: very soon, he would be just another human being; he would have to return to Earth, and wait eagerly for his mates to storm the European compound and rescue his parents. Then, with his family reunited — most of them, anyway — he would try to learn a trade or something like that, and find a job that didn't bore him too much. Perhaps he could become a history professor at Edinburgh University; Freja could surely pull some strings for him, especially in light of what he was giving up for humanity.

'*... us ... lius ...*'

Startled by the clipped sound, Julius sat up in his chair. He glanced at Ben, but he sat casually piloting the Heart, seemingly unaware of any strange occurrence.

'*... Julius ...*'

His eyes grew wide; there was no mistaking that it had been the voice of Professor Beloi. But what would he be doing out here? Had something happened? Maybe they had changed their plans, but then, why didn't they just hail them over the ship's com-link? He tried to clear his mind as best as he could, given the circumstances, and began searching for the voice, reaching out to it with his mind.

It wasn't long before Beloi found him again. '*Julius ... if you can hear me, don't say anything out loud ...*'

'*Professor? What are you doing here?*'

'*... trap ... don't use the Heart ... we're coming to get you ...*'

Julius was stunned. Please, say that is a joke, he thought, anything except that he had been lured into a trap. '*What ...*'

'*... don't use the Heart ... don't trust Hastings ...*' came the reply. Then the link was gone.

As Beloi's words hit home, Julius had a sudden moment of clarity, which made him blush in embarrassment. '*You are a complete and utter pillock, Julius and, quite frankly, you deserve everything that's coming to you,*' he thought bitterly to himself. With that out of his system, his mind clicked into gear again.

He tried to link back to Beloi, but failed. Still, his teacher had told him that they were coming for him, so he needed to stall Ben for as long as possible. 'Ben?' he said, trying to sound as if all was normal. 'How far are we from Arnesh?'

'Very close, actually. Are you curious to see the planet of your enemies?'

'Actually, yes I am. Too bad it'll be the last time.'

'It's sad having to lose all those brains,' continued Ben. 'Life could have been much more interesting if they had collaborated with us from the start. It would have benefited us all.'

'Sure,' said Julius. He began looking around the ship — which didn't take long, given its size — for anything that he could use to stop them from advancing. Faith would have come up with something, he was sure of that, but of course, he wasn't here. What could he do?

'Here we are, Julius,' said Ben.

Julius turned his head to look and saw it: the planet Arnesh, home of Queen Salgoria and all her subjects. It looked very much like a cloudless, smaller version of Earth, but with much less green to it. Land and sea were visible in equal measure, painting the surface brown and blue. He couldn't see any docking stations or fleet in its surrounding airspace, and wondered why that was.

Ben piloted the Heart steadily onwards, until they reached the planet's orbit, where he brought the vessel to a stop. Quickly, he reached for a panel to his right and began to type on it, before repeating the action on the Heart's main computer.

'What are you doing?' asked Julius.

'You'll see,' he answered, focusing on his preparations.

Suddenly, a field not dissimilar to the Zed Shield sprung into life, completely enclosing Arnesh. Promptly, a second one appeared, larger and thicker, which closed over the first one. Julius watched as the Heart slowly pierced the first layer, creating bright sparks of silver and gold, fizzling against the front of the ship. Once through, the craft came to a stop in the buffer zone between the two fields.

Ben relaxed in his chair. 'Great. Now we can talk in private. Beloi won't be able to link to you from the other side of this field.'

'What?' said Julius, alarmed.

'Let's stop pretending, shall we?' Ben replied, turning to face him. A cold glint was in his eyes. 'And, before you do anything stupid, think again, or someone else very dear to you will pay for it.'

As he said this, Julius heard a sound like a large panel swishing open, from the back of the Heart. He looked behind him, and saw a partition sliding down, revealing a small enclosure beyond it. Inside, was a glass container; from where he sat, he could just about discern the outline of a body within it. He stood and strode to it, a gasp escaping his lips as he got closer. There were in fact not one, but two bodies in the large container: those of Farrah and Michael, lying still side-by-side. Seeing her, he immediately remembered the scent from before — it was her perfume. She was so beautiful, and Julius felt a sudden pang of regret that almost knocked the breath out of him. He was overwhelmed by the urge to hold her and tell her how sorry he was for leaving her like he had.

As for Michael, he looked taller than the last time Julius had seen him, and he realised just how much he had missed his brother. 'What did you do to them?' he growled at Ben.

'Nothing, actually; they're just asleep, otherwise what kind of leverage would they be?'

Julius stormed back toward him, fury mounting within.

'As I was saying,' continued Ben, 'all I need to do is simply think about that red button inside their chamber, and it will open into space. Instant death!'

'You're lying,' said Julius, flatly. 'Arneshians don't have the skills for that.'

'Oh, but I'm not an Arneshian, Julius. I'm just like you — hence why I heard Beloi. I guess you were too shocked to realise that.' As he said this, he pointed his open palm at a medical kit, causing it to fly across the room with his mind skills. 'You believe me now?' The kit landed back on the shelf.

'Are you going to level with me, Ben?' asked Julius, sitting back down in his chair. With the hostages in danger, and for lack of a better plan, he decided to get Ben talking, hoping it would give enough time for his rescuers to reach them.

'Sure, I can spare a few moments while I set up here,' said Ben, approaching one of the terminals and setting to work on it. 'Salgoria needs to get rid of *all* of the Arneshians, and *you* are going to do it for her.'

'What?'

'Her people have become redundant, you see. Over the centuries, the impact of Tijara's attack with this machine, has had great repercussions on the entire population. The unaffected Arneshians mated with those who had lost their white pearls, diluting their abilities. Salgoria has always strived to create the most evolved species in the universe, and her new plan involves the Nuarns and a small group of pure Arneshians.'

'Where are they?'

'That is not your concern. All you need to focus on, is cleaning up that planet which, in case you've forgotten, is what the heads of Zed have always dreamt about. You'll be doing everyone a favour. And, if you're wondering, spreading the humans across the galaxy was just a way of keeping Zed busy, while I worked on the *real* hero of this mission: you.'

A thought occurred to Julius. 'How did you know I would go with you? What if I had gone to Freja instead? I almost did, you know? Your story would have been blown.'

Ben chuckled. It made Julius want to jump up and punch him in the face. 'To be honest, I'm surprised you *didn't*. I had another plan in place, again using your brother as leverage. Farrah was an added bonus, as were you, making my life easier by coming to me directly.'

Julius restrained himself, knowing his anger wouldn't help him right now. 'I won't do it. You can't make me.'

'True; but I'll tell you what I *can* do,' he said, continuing his preparations. 'I *can* kill Farrah, and I *can* kill Michael; I can even make sure Mielowa receives the proof that you killed K'Ssander last year.'

'Wha ... K'Ssander? No, I didn't!' cried Julius, stunned.

'I knew they wouldn't tell you, but I'm afraid he didn't survive the draw you did on him, who could, quite frankly? Anyway, Q&A time is over. Let's get to work. All I ask is that you use the Heart. Do that and you'll live through this — you'll *all* live through this,' he said, pointing at the back container. 'You have my word.'

Julius was at a loss for what to do. As his brain tried to cope with the news that he had willingly killed another person — because, in truth, he had *wanted* to kill K'Ssander — he realised that no rescue would reach him. He had run out of time and didn't doubt for one moment that Ben would kill his brother and Farrah. Could he risk challenging him to do it? No, he thought, he couldn't afford that. And even if he attacked him, Ben would only need a second to focus on the button in the container and all would be lost. He tried one last time to find Beloi with his mind, but he caught only static. Did it really have to end like this?

'Looks like the cavalry is here,' said Ben, sounding amused. 'You want to say hi?'

Behind the container, a back screen was revealed. Julius ran to it, his heart thumping hard in his chest. As he passed Farrah and Michael, his hope rekindled momentarily. At the back, he saw a fleet of ships, their outlines slightly blurred by the outer shield; at the head of them was the unmistakable nose of the Ahura Mazda. He fancied that he could just about make out the shapes of people behind the bridge, but that could merely have been wishful thinking. He wondered if they could see him, and he tried hard to link to Beloi and Kelly. The field dividing them must have been really strong however because, after several failed attempts, Julius had to give up. Kelly had found him in the end, but it was too late and, although it was a meager consolation, he knew that at least he would not be left to die alone. Suddenly, the noise of air escaping made him look down. With horror, he realised that Ben had lowered the partition of the glass container of a fraction, letting oxygen out into space. 'Wait!' he cried to Ben. 'I'll do it. Stop it!' The fissure closed up instantly.

'Place your hands here, Julius,' said Ben, inviting him to take a seat at the front. A glass pad had been uncovered on the main console. 'You really have no choice.'

At that moment, Julius knew that Hasting was right. He had accused Farrah of being selfish; now it was his time to show her what it truly meant to love someone. He turned away from the screen and trudged over to Ben. There, he sat down, opened his hands and gently lowered them over the glass control pad as directed, ignoring the ice-cold of its surface.

'It'll be over soon,' said Ben. He sat back down beside Julius and flicked a switch.

Julius felt the panel getting warmer, and a small blue light appeared below his hands. 'It looks like a crystal,' he thought. 'Like the one sketched on the door.' He couldn't feel any pain, as Ben had said, but his body was tingling all over, as if a low current, instead of blood, was now coursing through his veins.

'On the count of three, I want you to push hard against the glass,' said Ben. 'One ... Two ... Three.'

Julius took a deep breath and pushed. The heat beneath his hands intensified, making him wonder if he would have blisters afterwards. He was expecting something dramatic to occur, like flashes of light engulfing them, but nothing like that happened. He felt the hair on his body rise up, electrified, while his powers simply poured out of him, through his hands and into the Heart. More spectacular was what was happening outside the ship. A thick, yellow beam shot out towards Arnesh and, when it reached the inner field, closer to the planet's surface, it spread over it like a cocoon, in a dazzling flash of light.

It lasted just over a minute, before the voice of the computer came online: 'Transfer completed.'

Julius felt the flow diminishing, until it trickled down to nothing. The glass below his palm went cool and suddenly he felt incredibly tired. He collapsed in the chair, his hands flopping down into his lap. His head lolled to the side, and his eyes began to close, even as he fought against sleep. He forced them open a fraction. He could see Ben sliding the glass panel up, and gently lifting something blue from beneath it, before pocketing it. Whatever it was, it reflected the light like a prism. Julius tried hard to follow Ben's movement around the ship, but his head was heavy and kept lolling onto his chest. All sound had gone soft too, as if his ears had been stuffed with cotton. His eyes closed again.

Julius woke a little later, although he couldn't tell for sure how long he had been out, with fresh air blowing on his face. He was still in the Heart, sitting limply and with no strength to speak of. A light twitch had started in his legs, slowly working its way up. He couldn't understand why they were doing it, and that scared him. He realised that the air was coming from an open hatch. Julius tried to look in its direction by tilting his head a little. As he did so, he saw the shadow of someone standing on the threshold. It took him a few seconds but, as he lifted his head a little more and saw who it was, he gasped. Ambassador T'Rogon was there, holding the blue crystal object from the panel, high above his head, admiring it. Julius could hear footsteps drawing nearer, from behind him, and he saw first a pair of dangling, female boots then legs: Ben was carrying Farrah into the Arneshian vessel, which had docked with the Heart at some point while Julius had been asleep. T'Rogon looked greedily at the girl. Julius was desperate to leap up out of the chair and stop them, but he couldn't move. 'I'll find you, Farrah. I promise,' he whispered. He watched as Ben carried her away from him, leaving only her scent behind.

'Come,' said T'Rogon, looking to the back of the craft. 'He is spared, as promised.'

Julius didn't understand what T'Rogon meant; then a shadow fell over him and, when he looked up, he saw his brother.

'Now we're equal,' muttered Michael, leaning over him. He turned and moved over beside T'Rogon.

The Ambassador placed a hand on his shoulder and didn't move until the hatch between the two vessels had completely closed.

With that image etched in his mind, Julius passed out.

CHAPTER 12

A LONG SLEEP

'He's coming to.'

Julius opened his eyes and squinted against the light. As they adjusted, he noticed that there was a sheet of glass. He ran his eyes across its surface, and saw that it curved over him, disappearing into either side of the bed he was lying on. He tried to look down and examine himself, but found that he couldn't lift his head. What he saw however, was enough to get his heart beating fast. There were tubes filtering in and out of his arms and legs, with electrodes stuck to his chest; he couldn't feel his legs and a faint throbbing pulsated rhythmically in the back of his head. Beyond the glass he could see that he was in an unfamiliar place, possibly a sickbay, but not Tijara's. However, he did recognise Dr Walliser, when he leaned over the chamber and smiled at him.

'You'll need to be brief, Mizkis,' said the doctor, moving away.

The Skirts walked into Julius' view, and he thought that they looked quite drawn and pale, as well as scared.

Morgana placed her palms against the glass, fresh tears still smearing her cheeks. 'You stupid, stupid boy!' she cried suddenly. 'You could have died. What on Earth were you thinking?'

'I couldn't agree more,' said Freja's from behind them, out of view. His friends moved aside, and the Grand Master came to stand over him. He looked tired and gaunt. 'Did you really think me so ruthless as to send you off to sacrifice yourself like that, without a word, or any precautions?' said Freja, blankly.

He sounded disappointed, and to Julius that was worse than him just being upset.

'We know what happened,' continued Freja. 'The Heart's internal security cameras showed us everything.'

It was a relief to hear that, since he had no strength to explain himself, nor the skills to mind-talk to him anymore.

'I thought you'd be smarter than that. How could you believe him? Do you really think Ben would have been allowed to hurt Farrah? The daughter of Tijara and Arnesh is far too precious a gift to be airlocked at the whim of a traitor. Your brother is a Nuarn, a much needed breed in Salgoria's new world order; Ben told you so himself. And as for K'Ssander, he's alive and well. After he recovered from your draw, he was made to reveal the first location for our mission, which, in hindsight, was also part of T'Rogon's plan. That's why he was left behind in the first place.'

As Julius made sense of these words, he cursed his own stupidity.

'The only positive is that the Arneshians have no powers anymore — thanks to you — and their threat to us is now restricted to Salgoria and her elite group. But at what cost …'

Julius closed his eyes, trying to digest all of this.

'Salgoria wanted your powers all along,' said Freja, 'and Farrah's. Now she has both.' He was about to turn away, but stopped and looked at Julius, 'I thought we were family.'

Those words hit Julius harder than he could have believed possible, and silent tears began to fall from his face onto his pillow.

After Freja had left, no one moved for a while, until Dr Walliser came back to his patient, working fast at a terminal by the side of the chamber. 'Julius,' he called, 'the loss of your powers has greatly damaged your organs. The recovery will be long and painful. You have been placed into a stasis chamber, where you will sleep for some time. We are hopeful that this will accelerate the healing process.'

Julius mouthed the words, 'How long?'

Dr Walliser hesitated before answering. 'A few months should be sufficient.'

In response, Julius' tears increased, as he realised his impotence to say or do any differently.

'You must say your goodbyes now,' he said, turning to the Skirts.

They came forward, huddling around the chamber once more, and all put their palms on the glass. Julius could tell by their red eyes that Freja's news had affected them all.

'We'll find a way out of this, you'll see,' said Skye, trying to look tough.

'You just hibernate in there, WC,' said Faith. 'We'll take care of you this time.'

He felt so glad to have his friends there, that he temporarily forgot that he would never be a White Child again.

Lastly, he looked at Morgana. She sniffed first, then managed a smile, before her lips formed a few silent words. He wanted to ask her to repeat what she had said, to speak up, because he hadn't got it properly, and he felt somehow that it had been something very important. But a feeling of heaviness was overwhelming him, and he knew that the stasis was about to begin. So he just looked at her. It was the last image he saw before he fell into a deep sleep and for a long time, he knew no more.

About the Author

Francesca Tristan Barbini was born and raised in Rome, Italy, in 1976. After years of volunteer work around the world, she completed a MA Honour in Religious Studies at New College, Edinburgh, focusing on the Ancient Near East and the Dead Sea Scrolls.

Her free time is divided between family, painting RPG miniatures and writing books for children and adults. An active member of the Tolkien Society, she also runs a kinship on Lord of the Rings Online. Barbini is currently working on the fifth instalment of her Tijaran Tales series.

For more information please see **www.ftbarbini.com**.

THE ADVENTURE CONTINUES...

BOOK 1

WHITE CHILD: When 12 year old Julius McCoy is told that he has been selected to join the elite Zed Lunar Academy, he is over the moon...literally. It promises to be a year of neck-breaking races in The Hologram Palace, spaceship-pilot training and of course, developing his own very special mind-skills.

Yet even as he begins to get a grip on his fantastic abilities, strange things start to happen around him. Who are the three mysterious men hanging about in Satras, the moon capital - particularly their sinister leader in the red cap, who seems to know a lot more than he should about Julius?

And what of the growing threat of the evil Queen Salgoria, head of the technologically-gifted Arneshian outcasts, who are making ominous advances again? It's all a lot more than a young boy should be expected to deal with. Yet, little does Julius realise exactly how critical he will be to the fate of Zed, and ultimately, Earth itself.

BOOK 2

THE ORACLE OF LIFE: 13 year old Julius McCoy is about to start his second year at Tijara Academy, in the Zed Lunar Perimeter. With the threat of the Arneshians averted for the moment, he can get on with the important part of his school life: developing his rare mind-skills.

Of course, what any student on Zed looks forward to most, is gaming in the Hologram Palace. But who is the mysterious lady hidden in one of the games? This encounter will set in motion an exciting and dangerous treasure hunt, that will give him a whole new perspective on the real history of Zed, and ultimately beyond, to a shocking truth that could jeopardise the safety of everyone he holds dear.

When an old enemy returns, it becomes clear that the Arneshians are back with a new plan for taking over Zed and seizing control of Earth. As the pieces of the puzzle fall into place, and he is drawn towards a climactic showdown, it will take all of Julius' mind-skills as he is forced into a deadly final duel.

BOOK 3

THE NUARN RIFT: Fourteen year old Julius McCoy is about to start his third year at the Zed Lunar Academy.

He's in for a major surprise too, as Earth's old enemies, the Arneshians, make a sudden reappearance, this time carrying a banner of peace and reconciliation.

But there's an even bigger shock in store for him, with a startling revelation much closer to home.